THE NORA NOTEBOOKS

THE TROUBLE WITH

THE NORA NOTEBOOKS

THE TROUBLE WITH
ANTS

Book 1

CLAUDIA MILLS

Illustrated by Katie Kath

Alfred A. Knopf New York

THIS IS A BORZOI BOOK PUBLISHED BY ALFRED A. KNOPF

Visit us on the Web! randomhousekids.com

Educators and librarians, for a variety of teaching tools, visit us at RHTeachersLibrarians.com

Library of Congress Cataloging-in-Publication Data
Mills, Claudia.
The trouble with ants / Claudia Mills ; Illustrated by Katie Kath Boyd. — First edition.
pages cm. — (The Nora notebooks ; book 1)
Summary: "Science-obsessed fourth grader Nora wants to be like her scientist family and publish a professional research paper on her favorite subject: her ant farm!"—Provided by publisher
ISBN 979-0-385-39161-0 (trade) — ISBN 978-0-385-39162-7 (lib. bdg.) — ISBN 978-0-385-39164-1 (ebook)
[1. Ants—Fiction. 2. Science—Fiction. 3. Friendship—Fiction. 4. Schools—Fiction.] I. Kath, Katie, illustrator. II. Title.
PZ7.M63963Ts 2015
[Fic]—dc23
2015007380

The text of this book is set in 12.5-point New Aster.

Printed in the United States of America
September 2015
10 9 8 7 6 5 4 3 2 1

First Edition

To the incomparable Nancy Hinkel,
who caused this book to be

−C.M.

Nora Alpers woke up early on New Year's morning and reached for the handsome leather-bound notebook she had gotten for Christmas. The notebook had a magnetic clasp that closed with a highly satisfying *click*.

"You can use it for a diary," Nora's mother had suggested.

Nora had no intention of using the notebook as a diary. She planned on writing more interesting things in it than "Today, I had breakfast. Then I went to school. Then I went home."

"You can write stories in it," her older sister had teased. Sarah was a grown-up geologist who was expecting her first baby in a couple of months. Like everyone in Nora's family, Sarah knew Nora preferred nonfiction to fiction.

"Or poetry." Her brother, Mark, who was studying electrical engineering at MIT, had given Nora a grin.

Only her father had understood. "Nora is going to use her notebook," he had said, obviously offering a prediction, not a suggestion, "for writing down fascinating facts about ants."

Her father was absolutely, completely right.

Nora loved scribbling down all kinds of facts in all kinds of notebooks: big ones, little ones, fat ones, skinny ones, spiral ones, and now this new super-fancy one.

She had waited to start her new notebook on the first day of the new year.

"Fascinating Facts About Ants," she now wrote on the first blank page with her blue ballpoint pen. But she might write fascinating facts about other subjects, too. "And Other Extremely Interesting Things," she added.

She'd write facts she'd learned from the ant

books she checked out of the grown-up section of the library. Even better, she'd write facts she had discovered all by herself by doing experiments on the ants in her very own ant farm.

Did they accomplish more tunnel building when they were warm or cold? (Warm.) Did they build more quickly in the dark or the light? (It didn't seem to matter.) Right now she was investigating whether they dug faster in dry or wet sand. She had poured 30 milliliters (about an eighth of a cup) of water into the ant farm yesterday: not enough to drown her ants, of course, just enough to increase the moisture content of the sand. So far, they seemed to be having a harder time tunneling through the wet sand, probably because the water made it heavier. At least that was her current hypothesis.

She still had the notes she had made from her past experiments that she could copy into her notebook. And she'd learn new facts to add all the time.

This would be the Year of the Ant!

Nora thought about the Chinese calendar, which had twelve different years. It had mostly mammals in it: Year of the Rat, Ox, Tiger, Rabbit, Horse, Goat, Monkey, Dog, Pig. It had one reptile: Year of the Snake. It had one bird: Year of the Rooster. It even had one imaginary creature: Year of the Dragon. Nora didn't approve of the Year of the Dragon at all, not that you could expect scientific accuracy from astrology.

The Chinese had no year of any insect at all. No Year of the Grasshopper. No Year of the Bee. No Year of the Cockroach. If Nora had been in charge of the Chinese zodiac, she would have replaced the Year of the Dragon with the Year of the Dragonfly.

And now her own personal calendar was launching the Year of the Ant, or rather, the Year of Many, Many Ants.

Nora rummaged through her current ant library book to find an especially amazing ant fact to use as the first fact in her new notebook.

Nora's own Year of the Ant had begun.

Later that afternoon, Nora sat examining her friend Brody Baxter through the wrong end of the telescope she had gotten as another Christmas present. Brody appeared to be very tiny, very far away, and trying to get his dog to hold several tennis balls at once in his mouth.

Brody was actually a somewhat short but basically normal-sized fourth grader, seated on the floor right next to Nora in her family room. But he was indeed trying to coax his dog to fill his mouth with tennis balls.

"Just try, Dog," Brody pleaded as Dog—that was the dog's name—dropped a tennis ball onto the carpet. "The world record is five, and you're the best dog in the world, so I know you can do six."

Dog appeared to disagree. So far, he hadn't managed to hold more than one. Tennis balls scattered.

Nora set down her telescope and retrieved a tennis ball that had rolled under the couch. Her other friend who had come to visit, Mason Dixon, collected a ball that had bounced over to the table where Nora's ant farm stood. The ants didn't seem to be noticing the tennis ball commotion.

Mason and Brody were best friends and co-owners of Dog, although Dog had to live at Mason's house because of Brody's father's terrible allergies. As far as Nora could tell, both boys loved Dog equally, but Brody was vastly more enthusiastic about earning Dog a Guinness World Record. Then again, Brody was vastly more enthusiastic than Mason about everything.

"Maybe there's a different record you could try to break," Nora suggested.

From where it had been lying on the floor, she picked up the *Guinness World Records* that Brody had gotten as his favorite Christmas present and used the index to find records involving dogs. She loved books with indexes.

"'Longest tongue,'" she read aloud. "Eleven point four three centimeters. That doesn't sound *that* long."

Mason and Brody stared at her blankly. They weren't scientists the way she was; they didn't measure things using the metric system. "Four and a half inches," she translated. "Do you think Dog's tongue could be longer than four and a half inches?"

"No," said Mason.

"Yes!" said Brody. "Dog, stick out your record-breaking tongue!"

Dog was still panting enough from his tennis ball efforts that his tongue hung out partway. Nora studied what she could see of it. There was no way that Dog's tongue was four and a half inches, let alone longer. Also, where were they supposed to measure it *from*? Where did his tongue *start*? She retrieved a ruler from the drawer in the ant farm's table, because she knew Brody wouldn't believe her otherwise.

"You hold his tongue, and I'll measure," Brody told Mason.

"How about *you* hold his tongue, and *I'll* measure?" Mason countered.

"Sure." Brody was always agreeable. "I'll stretch it out as long as I can. Dog won't mind, not if he gets a world record out of it, right, Dog?"

Dog allowed Brody to hold his tongue out to its full length, but it was clear to Nora that Mason had no idea how he was supposed to go about measuring it.

"Not even close," Mason finally concluded. "Maybe three inches? It's hard to tell."

"What other records are there?" Brody asked Nora. "Pinkest tongue? Wettest tongue? Lickingest tongue?"

Nora closed the book, keeping her finger in the dog record section. In her opinion, Dog's tongue needed a rest before the boys began testing anything else about it. It was time to change the subject.

"My favorite Christmas present was my telescope. Well, my telescope and my new ant notebook. Brody's was his *Guinness World Records* book. What about you, Mason?"

"My *least* favorite was a harmonica. Tied with a book on how to juggle."

"How could your parents think you'd want to play the harmonica? Or learn to juggle?" Nora asked. "You don't like doing new things."

"*I* know that. And *they* know that. But they keep on hoping."

"Could we teach Dog to juggle?" Brody asked, with new excitement.

"No," Nora and Mason said together.

"Dog has three legs," Mason reminded Brody.

That was one of the reasons Mason and Brody

had adopted him, because nobody else had wanted to take him home from the animal shelter.

"He doesn't need four legs to juggle," Brody said. "He'll juggle with his front legs and his mouth, and he'll be the best dog juggler in the world!"

Nora sighed. She would never understand other people and their pets. Mason, who hardly liked anything, was wild about Dog. Brody, who loved everything, loved Dog most of all. Emma Averill, in their class at school, had a cat named Precious Cupcake—Nora shuddered at the name—who starred in endless cat videos Emma showed everyone on her cell phone. Emma was the only fourth grader Nora knew who had a cell phone of her own. In the most recent video, before winter break, Precious Cupcake had been wearing a Santa Claus hat while being made to dance to "Jingle Bell Rock."

Nora's gaze fell fondly on her ant farm. Ants were such sensible pets. They didn't wear comical hats or do holiday dances. They stayed content in their tidy glass enclosure: independent, self-reliant, busy, and endlessly interesting.

"All right," Nora said, turning back to the *Guinness* book. "Here's another dog record: how many steps can a dog walk while balancing a cup of water on his head without spilling it?"

Brody leaped to his feet. "Do you have a glass? Will your parents mind if we spill a little water?"

"Dog has three legs," Mason reminded Brody again. "Walking with a cup of water on your head is harder if you don't have as many legs as other people—I mean, other dogs."

Brody's already bright face brightened even more. "*That* can be the record! Most steps taken with a glass of water balanced on the head of a dog with three legs!"

Nora shook her head. "That's too *specific* a record. Too narrow a category. There aren't enough three-legged dogs carrying glasses of water on their heads for it to be worth setting a record about."

"So what else is there?" Brody persisted.

Nora shrugged. She had already flipped to the section on ants. There was a record for largest ant farm, but what kind of a dumb record was that? What did the *size* of an ant farm matter? It was what ants *did* in their farm that counted. And even if her ants proved to be faster at tunnel building than other people's ants, that wouldn't be what

Nora cared about. She'd want to know *why* they were so fast. It was the science behind the record that was worth thinking about. *Why* did one dog have such a long tongue? *How* did another dog carry so many tennis balls in its mouth or balance a glass of water so carefully on its head?

"Maybe we need to come up with our own record," Brody suggested. "Not a record that's already in the book for Dog to break, but a new record that nobody ever thought up before."

"Like what?" Mason sounded skeptical.

"Like—like—Nora, you're really good at thinking things up."

It was true. But, frankly, Nora greatly doubted that there was anything at all that Dog was best in the world at doing. After all, it couldn't be easy to be best in the world at something, or else everyone would be that good, and then it wouldn't be *best* anymore.

"Can Dog learn how to play the harmonica?" Brody asked.

"No," Nora and Mason said together.

Nora kept on thumbing through the pages of Brody's book. It was amazing how many records people held for all kinds of strange things: largest collection of rubber ducks, most spoons balanced on the face, farthest distance to spit milk.

She hoped Brody wouldn't decide to train Dog in milk spitting, at least not this afternoon, at her house.

Then her eyes fell upon another world record: youngest person ever to have a research paper published in a peer-reviewed science journal. The person was a girl named Emily Rosa. Emily Rosa had been eleven when she published her record-breaking paper.

Nora was ten.

She hardly listened as Brody asked Mason if Dog could get a record for *chewing* tennis balls, given that Dog had already destroyed two tennis balls in the last half hour.

Had Emily Rosa loved science since she had been old enough to love anything?

Did Emily Rosa have the periodic table of the elements and a map of all the constellations, both Northern and Southern Hemispheres, hanging on the wall of her bedroom?

Did Emily Rosa know how to fix a broken vacuum cleaner?

Did Emily Rosa have her own telescope?

Nora had already done months of experiments with her ant farm and documented them all in a special science notebook. She was probably already the leading ten-year-old expert on myrmecology, the scientific study of ants. She had been looking for a worthy goal for the new year, and now she had found it: to be the youngest person ever to publish an article in a grown-up science journal.

She glanced over again at her busy, bustling ants, burrowing through their nicely moistened sand. They had no idea how important they were soon going to be to the future of science.

A worker ant is less than one-millionth the size of a human being. But all of the ants in the world taken together weigh as much as all the human beings in the world. See what I mean about how amazing ants are?

School started again the next day. Nora didn't mind that winter break was over. She liked her fourth-grade teacher, an enthusiastic, sports-loving man who called himself Coach Joe. Coach Joe had told Nora once that he'd like her to bring her ant farm to school to show their class. Maybe she should plan to do that soon.

As she stood outside Plainfield Elementary School in the early-morning cold waiting for the bell, she heard a shriek.

"Dunk! Stop that! Dunk! No!"

Nora recognized that shriek. It could belong to only one shrieker: Emma Averill.

Dunk, the biggest, beefiest boy in their class, had scooped up a handful of snow from the shoveled mounds by the side of the blacktop.

"Here's some nice clean snow, Emma!" he called out, holding up his snowball for all to see. "Your face looks a little dirty. Don't you think it could use a good washing?"

Emma shrieked again. It wasn't a bloodcurdling shriek, more of a cross between a shriek and a giggle.

Mason and Brody had arrived, inseparable as usual, joining the crowd of Coach Joe's fourth graders surrounding Dunk and Emma.

"Why is Dunk picking on Emma?" Brody asked indignantly.

"Because he's mean," Mason replied.

Nora stared at both of them. Hadn't they seen any shows on the Animal Planet channel? Boy penguins made strange cries and flapped their flippers to attract girl penguins. Boy lions ruffled their manes to attract girl lions. And boy humans threatened to wash the faces of girl humans with handfuls of snow.

"Dunk is acting that way because he *likes* Emma," Nora explained. "And Emma is shrieking so loudly because she likes Dunk."

Brody looked doubtful. Mason looked shocked. Nora knew Mason was thinking: *how could* anybody *like* Dunk?

The bell rang. Nora made her way into Coach Joe's room, Emma's shrieks still ringing in her ears.

Coach Joe's class always began with a "huddle" on the football-shaped rug in the back corner of the room.

"Welcome back, team!" Coach Joe said. "Everyone ready for some championship play? Grand slams? Slam dunks?" He grinned at Dunk, who had wedged himself next to Emma. "Touchdowns?"

Coach Joe clearly liked sports metaphors. Nora herself played on a YMCA basketball team with Mason, Brody, and her friends Elise, Tamara, and Amy. Elise loved writing the way Nora loved science. Tamara loved jazz dance and hip-hop. Amy, who wanted to be a vet someday, loved animals, though Nora hadn't been able to convince Amy to share her own fondness for ants. All of them loved basketball, even if their team, the Fighting Bulldogs, really should have been named the Losing Bulldogs.

The other kids clapped in response to Coach Joe's greeting, except for Mason, who didn't go in for clapping. Nora wasn't a big clapper, either, but she gave a nod of approval. It would definitely be a grand slam, slam dunk, and touchdown when she published an article about her ants in a grown-up science journal.

"Social studies!" Coach Joe went on. "So far this school year, we've learned about Native Americans, the age of exploration, and the settling of the thirteen colonies. So you know what's coming, don't you?"

Most of Nora's classmates looked blank.

Someone had to say something, so she raised her hand.

"The American Revolution."

"Exactly!" Coach Joe beamed at Nora, as if she had said something brilliant instead of the most obvious thing in the world. "The Sons of Liberty.

The Boston Tea Party. Battles. More battles. The Declaration of Independence. Washington crossing the Delaware. The terrible winter at Valley Forge. Yes, pretty soon we're going to see our colonists with a brand-new country."

Leaning toward Emma, Dunk gave a loud burp that he clearly thought any fourth-grade girl would find irresistible.

"Dunk," Coach Joe said, without even casting a look in his direction.

The burping ceased.

"In language arts," Coach Joe continued, "we'll be taking a page from the colonists' playbook and writing our own persuasive speeches. The revolution wasn't won primarily with muskets and cannons, you know. It was won with words. 'These are the times that try men's souls.' 'Give me liberty or give me death.' 'We hold these truths to be self-evident, that all men are created equal.'"

Nora didn't think of herself as a word person—she planned to write her ant farm article in plain, simple words that told about her ant experiments in a plain, simple way—but the stirring lines Coach Joe had quoted did give her a strange, shimmery feeling inside. She could see how they could make someone feel like launching a revolution.

"So we'll be working on learning how to write our own persuasive speeches," Coach Joe concluded.

"What are we going to be trying to persuade people to do?" Mason asked. Nora knew Mason was tired of listening to speeches from his parents, which were intended to persuade him to try new things.

"Anything you like," Coach Joe replied. "You can pretend to be a colonist and help the cause of rebellion. You can pretend to be a Tory and defend the rule of King George the Third. You can write a persuasive letter to your congressional representative. After all, we wouldn't even have congressional representatives if it weren't for the persuasive speeches of the American Revolution. How about a speech to convince your parents to let you stay up late to watch your favorite TV show? Or a speech to convince me to give you less homework—good luck on that one! Write about whatever matters most to *you*."

Nora didn't know yet what she'd write about.

She did know that her persuasive speech would rely on facts—hard, cold, true facts—rather than on fancy phrases. She wouldn't write lines like "Give me liberty or give me death." She'd list the pros and cons of liberty, and the pros and cons of death, and count up the pros and cons on each side, and see which side added up to the biggest number. Nothing was more persuasive than math.

"All right, team," Coach Joe said. "Huddle's over. Time for the back-to-school after-winter-break kickoff."

At lunch, Nora sat with the other girls on her basketball team, as well as with Emma and Emma's best friend, Bethy. She would have sat with Mason and Brody sometimes, but in the cafeteria at Plainfield Elementary School, fourth-grade girls and fourth-grade boys never sat together. There was no rule that said it had to be that way, but everyone seemed to know that was how it had to be.

Nora understood. In the animal kingdom, the females of many species lived separately from the males for much of the time: seals, elk, mink. On the other hand, no female member of the animal kingdom ever expected another female member of the animal kingdom to squeal over her latest cat videos.

As Nora carried her tray over to their table, Bethy was hunched together with Tamara, Elise, and Amy, all peering at the tiny screen on Emma's phone. Plainfield Elementary had a rule against calling or texting during school hours, but apparently there was no policy against using your phone at lunchtime to make other people watch videos of your cat.

"Oh!" Bethy gushed.

"That's not even the cutest one," Emma announced, taking control of her phone. "The cutest one—wait till you see it—the cutest one is the one I'm calling 'Princess Precious.' Okay, here it is."

Beaming, Emma handed the phone back to Bethy so that the other girls could resume their peering.

"I love her cape!" Elise gave a sigh of admiration.

"Pink is definitely her color," Tamara agreed.

Amy exchanged a glance with Nora; Nora knew

Amy didn't approve of costumes for pets. But Amy asked politely, "Where did you find a cat tiara?"

All the girls seemed to act differently around Emma. Nora would hardly recognize them as the same girls who could knock a basketball out of someone else's hands and barrel down the court for a layup.

But right here, right now, there was no escaping Precious Cupcake. Nora leaned in closer to behold Emma's cat dressed in a jeweled beauty-queen crown and a cape of pink velvet trimmed with purple ribbon.

"What breed of cat is she?" Nora asked. Probably American shorthair. Amy looked eager to hear the answer to Nora's question, too.

Emma shrugged, obviously less interested in the biological classification of her cat than in her costumed cuteness.

"They should put her picture in the dictionary next to the word *cute*!" Bethy exclaimed.

"Here's another one," Emma said. "I'm calling this one 'Cupcake Capers.' I take back what I said before: *this* one is the cutest."

Out of the corner of her eye, Nora caught a

glimpse of Precious Cupcake licking the frosting off an actual cupcake. Not a healthy food choice for cats, that was for sure. But even future vet Amy made no comment.

"Nora, you can see it first this time," Emma told her.

"That's okay," Nora said. "I don't mind waiting."

Maybe the end-of-lunch bell would ring before it was her turn to admire the Cupcake Capers of Precious Cupcake. Luckily, right now the squealers were too busy squealing to notice that she wasn't squealing, too. So Nora gratefully tuned out the

gushing and sighing of her friends, and sat thinking of more fascinating facts about ants that she
could write in her special notebook.

The total population of ants in the world
is ten thousand trillion. To write a number
that big, you'd have to write a one
followed by 16 zeroes! Which looks like this:
10,000,000,000,000,000.

It was hard now for Nora to remember a time when she didn't have an ant farm. But actually it had been only a few months ago that ants first came into her life in a serious way.

She had always liked watching ants in nature. She'd be out on a walk on a summer afternoon, and there on the sidewalk would be a swarm of ants, thousands of them, crowded so thickly together that half a square of concrete was black with them. Why were they there now, when they hadn't been there a day ago? Had an ant scout located some unexpected treat or danger, and alerted the others? How did they communicate? What kinds of things did they communicate about?

Toward the end of third grade, her parents had helped her order an ant farm on the Internet, along with a tube of ants.

Nora had studied the website that described what they'd be getting.

"'Live arrival guaranteed,'" she read to her mother as she sat at the computer in her mother's office at the university. Both her parents were scientists. Her dad was a biochemist, and her mother was an astrophysicist. They joked that he liked to study tiny things very close up and she liked to study enormous things very far away.

Nora kept on reading from the ant farm website.

"But they say they can guarantee live arrival only if the temperature isn't below forty degrees or above eighty-five. How hot is it going to be"—she checked the estimated delivery date if she placed her order today—"three days from now?"

Her mother pulled up the weather on her phone. "High of eighty-six. What do you think? Take a chance on them anyway?"

Nora knew that the hopeful look in her mother's

eyes meant that she wanted Nora's answer to be no. Her mother, who was one of the country's foremost scientific experts on the rings of Saturn, had a most unscientific aversion to bugs, including ladybugs, which even Emma didn't mind.

Nora nodded. "I want to go ahead and order them. Now that it's almost summer, it's only going to be getting hotter and hotter."

Her ants were just going to have to deal with the weather, whatever it was. After all, ants lived outside in the world in all temperatures, freezing cold to blazing hot. Of course, in the outside world they lived underground in their snug little tunnels. Still, Nora was sure she had seen ants swarming on the pavement on days when the temperature soared past eighty-five degrees.

She did feel nervous three days later, when she came home from school and retrieved the small carton from the mailbox.

Would her ants be alive or dead?

"Be alive!" she beamed the command toward the package, even though she knew she couldn't make any difference in their aliveness just by willing it with all her might.

In the kitchen, she cut through the tape on the

box with a pair of shears and opened the lid. From a heap of Styrofoam peanuts, she pulled out the plastic ant farm, a bit disappointed by how silly it looked, with its green plastic houses, barn, silo, and windmill. As if ants would care about any of that! An ant farm wasn't really a *farm*. No one had ever sung *"E-I-E-I-O"* about ants. At least Nora was pretty sure that was the case.

Where *were* the ants?

Digging deeper into the Styrofoam peanuts, she grasped a small tube.

Filled with ants.

Filled with ants that were . . . alive! Ants that were not only alive but apparently eager to get out. Ants that, in fact, looked quite angry—not that Nora believed you could attribute human emotions to ants. But if you could, if ants did have the same feelings that people did, these ants resembled people who were very, very irritated at having spent the last few days in uncomfortably warm temperatures, cooped up in a little plastic tube.

The instructions said to put the ants in the re-frigerator for ten minutes to calm them down before transferring them into their new home. They'd probably enjoy that anyway.

The instructions said that the ants in the tube were western harvester ants.

The instructions also said that western harvester ants were stinging ants.

"Dad," Nora said as her father wandered into the kitchen to refill his coffee cup. "They sent us stinging ants. The instructions say that my ants 'can inflict a painful sting.'"

Her dad looked sober, even though he was a fellow insect lover. "Your mother isn't wild about ants to start with," he said in a low voice. "I don't think she's going to be pleased with the idea of stinging ants."

"What am I not going to be pleased with?" came Nora's mother's voice from the kitchen doorway.

"Oh, nothing. Look, Mom, they're here!" Nora made her own voice cheerful, so her mother would get into the proper ant-loving mood. "My ants are here, and they *are* alive!"

"Oh goody," her mother replied.

Neither Nora nor her father made any mention about painful stings.

"So where are they?" her mother asked uneasily.

Nora held up the tube. Her mother shrank back, as if the ants might leap out and start marching all over the kitchen, bent on conquest.

"We need to put them in the fridge first," Nora explained, "to calm them down."

"Well, I do greatly prefer calm ants to agitated ones," her mother said. "But ants in the refrigerator? I can't believe it's healthy to put a tube of ants right next to our family's food supply."

"They won't get out," Nora reassured her.

"Says who?"

"Says me. They can't get out. Look, the stopper is in nice and tight."

To demonstrate, Nora turned the ant tube upside down to show how snugly the stopper was in place.

"Oh, Nora, I really don't think—"

"It's fine! Mom, the ant company isn't going to ship ants in a tube with a loose stopper." *Especially painfully stinging ants.*

For a further demonstration, Nora wiggled the stopper a bit and then gave the upside-down tube of ants a good shake.

"See?"

But what she saw next, what they all saw, was the stopper popping out.

Large red ants—large, red, seemingly angry stinging ants—scattered all over the kitchen floor.

Nora's mother screamed.

"Catch them! Nora! Neil! Catch them!"

It would definitely be a good idea to catch them. On that, Nora and her mother were in complete agreement. The question was: how?

For the next twenty minutes, Nora and her father tried to collect the ants, one by one, scooping them into empty jars from the recycling bin. But the ants didn't want to be scooped. And sometimes one that had already been scooped became unscooped and made its way out as another ant was being coaxed to make its way in.

Nora's mother had fled to the safety of the dining room. She kept calling unhelpful things like "Be sure you get them all!" and "It's all right just to kill them if you need to!"

Nora was trying to tune out this unwelcome advice when one of the painfully stinging ants gave a painful sting to the tip of her index finger.

"Ow!" she couldn't help but yell. "Ow!"

"What is it? What happened?" her mother called.

"It's okay," her father called back.

"It doesn't sound okay."

Her mother reappeared in the kitchen doorway as Nora was sucking her stung finger.

Concern for Nora gave her mom new courage. Heedless of any remaining escaped ants, she rushed over to examine Nora's finger.

"Oh, this looks bad. What kind of ants *are* these?"

When no one answered, she snatched up the instructions from the counter. "*Stinging ants?* They sent you *stinging* ants?"

That had definitely been a terrible afternoon.

Nora's father took over as the sole ant re-capturer, leaving Nora's mother to administer first aid for the sting. In the end, twenty ants were deposited into the ant farm, to settle into the soft white sand that Nora had already put in place to welcome them, moistened with a quarter cup of water. The few remaining ants were never seen again, except for one that provoked a scream from her mother a day or two later and got itself squished to death with a wadded paper towel.

Holding no hard feelings toward her ants—you couldn't blame a stinging ant for stinging any more than you could blame a singing bird for singing— Nora did her best to care for them, giving them little bits of apple or cracker to eat and making sure they had a few drops of water to drink every couple of days.

For the first week, the ants did all the things that Nora had hoped they would do: they built tunnels, carried morsels of food off to eat and digest, stayed busy in useful ant ways.

But then they started dying. And kept on dying. And soon they were all dead.

Maybe Nora had fed them too much or too little? Or maybe they were just at the end of their life expectancy. Without a queen, they couldn't reproduce and create new baby ants to keep the colony going. The instructions had said that it was against the law for the ant farm company to send a queen through the mail. Nora had no idea who would make a law like that, or why.

Her ants were dead and done for. But Nora wasn't done with ants.

On the Internet, she learned that she could make

34

her own ant farm, using a rectangular, flat terrarium from a pet or craft store. She could use dirt from her own backyard. And she could find her own ants to live in it.

She had no trouble finding ants. Nora was good at noticing things like where dirt was mounded in a corner of the yard to form an anthill. It was harder finding a queen: the large, winged ant that hatched all the eggs that became all the ants that would keep the colony going. Queens didn't sit out in plain view on ant-sized thrones, with ant-sized crowns on their heads. They were hidden deep inside the colony, protected by soldier ants. No matter how long she watched and waited, Nora never saw any queen ready for capture.

Maybe it would have been wrong to capture a queen anyway. Maybe that's why ant farm companies weren't allowed to ship queens through the mail. The other ants would be asking, "Where's our queen? Where did she go? Oh, Your Majesty, what has become of you?"

No. Ants didn't ask questions like that. They didn't really think at all. Their brains were too small for thinking. In any case, Nora never found a queen.

But her second colony of ants lived longer than the first, mail-order colony of ants. And when they died off, she just went out and found more.

And now she was ready for her year of serious scientific ant experiments to begin.

Ant queens live a long time. The queens of most species live 5 years or longer. The record for a queen's life span is 30 years! But lots of queens die before they ever get to found a colony. For every queen that succeeds in starting a colony, hundreds or thousands die trying. I would love to have an ant queen someday more than anything in the world.

As soon as she got to her house that afternoon, Nora checked on her ants. Some days, she took the bus from school to a parent's office at the university and did homework there until they were ready to leave. On other days, one parent was working at home, grading exams or doing something on the computer, so she could walk home directly from school. This was a walk-home day.

Whenever she checked her ant farm after a whole day away at school, she always found that something had changed. New tunnels had appeared.

Food had been eaten. A deceased ant had been carried off to the corner of the farm where her ants stored their dead.

Today, she arrived home halfway through an ant funeral. Two ants were lugging the corpse of a third down a long tunnel to reach the ant graveyard.

Rest in peace, little ant.

Nora considered recording the ant burial with her parents' old video camera. *That* would be something to show the other girls at lunch tomorrow. *That* would be a pleasant change from the Precious Cupcake costume parade. But she wasn't going to let herself start imitating Emma, even if Amy might enjoy a change in video subjects, too.

It might be a good idea, however, to start documenting her ants' activities. She could record them for the sake of science, not for lunchtime show-and-tell. If she studied the videos, she might get an idea for her groundbreaking experiment. She couldn't publish a scientific article on the usual science-fair stuff that any kid with an ant farm had already found on ant farm websites. She had to come up with something that science had never seen before.

Nora filmed her ants for a while. Then she did homework: some easy math problems, and reading a chapter in her huge social studies textbook on the American Revolution. She already knew that she wasn't going to be reading about any women who did important things to help the cause of freedom. Most of the famous women back then were famous because they were married to famous men. That wasn't how Nora planned on becoming famous as a scientist.

Neither of her parents were really famous scientists, but her mother was more famous than her father, even if her father kept a calmer, more scientific head when stinging western harvester ants were on the loose in the kitchen. Her mother was on TV occasionally, when the rings of Saturn made the national news. Admittedly, that wasn't often. If Nora were in charge of the news, she'd lead off every night with stories like "New Discovery About the Chemical Composition of Stars!" and "Breakthrough in Ant Farm Research!"

Maybe that's what she should write her persuasive speech about: why the news should have more science stories.

Emma would probably write hers about how the news should have more cat videos.

Nora smiled at the thought.

But then her smile disappeared. Even if her speech was a better speech, her classmates would probably end up being more persuaded by Emma's. Persuasive speeches could only go so far and do so much. First, people had to be willing to be persuaded.

It was definitely time for her to bring her farm to school to show Coach Joe's class the wonder of ants.

The next day and the day after that, it was unseasonably warm for January, with highs in the sixties.

Global climate change, Nora thought to herself darkly.

But warmer temperatures were good for transporting an ant farm to school. She had confirmed with Coach Joe that she could present her ant farm during science on Friday. Ants had nothing to do with electromagnetism, their current subject of study, but Coach Joe said ants would make a nice change.

"Kids will still get a *charge* out of them," he told Nora.

She was so surprised to hear him making a science pun rather than a sports reference that she forgot to give a polite chuckle.

Nora's father drove her to school on Friday so she wouldn't jostle her ant farm or risk tripping and shattering months of her ants' hard work. She kept the farm covered with an old T-shirt. While she didn't think of herself as a dramatic person, she wanted to introduce her ants to the class with some fanfare. She suspected that a lot of people, unbelievable as it might seem, thought ants were boring.

Ants? Boring?!

So she wanted the equivalent of a drumroll before she uncovered the farm to their astonished eyes.

She didn't wait on the blacktop for the bell. Instead, she hurried to Coach Joe's room and set the ant farm safely on the bookcase in the back of the room, where it wouldn't be disturbed.

Coach Joe was at his desk when she arrived.

"The ants go marching two by two, hurrah, hurrah!" he sang out in greeting.

Nora had forgotten about that kindergarten song. She was glad there was a song about ants, but of course the ants in the song did the most un-ant-like things imaginable. "The little one stops to suck his thumb." As if ants had thumbs rather than mandibles! "The little one stops to tie his shoe." Tying a shoe? Really?

Still, Nora gave Coach Joe a smile. He meant well.

"Nora, I'm thinking it might work better to let you show your ants during the morning huddle. What do you think?"

"Sure," Nora agreed. Now that her ants were here at school, the sooner she could show them to everybody, the better.

Maybe Emma would want to start taking ant videos? Or at least watching them once in a while? Wouldn't that be a lovely change at lunchtime?

The bell rang. Nora's audience came racing into Coach Joe's room, Dunk leading the way with his shouts and swagger.

One tiny worry wormed itself into Nora's brain.

Dunk had a tendency to be a bully. He'd better not even think about bullying her ants!

Once morning announcements had been read, the Pledge of Allegiance recited, and "You're a Grand Old Flag" sung, Coach Joe called the class into their Friday huddle. Nora carried the T-shirt-covered object from the bookcase to the football-shaped rug. She sat down and settled it safely on her lap, stroking its T-shirt cover as if to reassure her ants before their big moment.

"What's that?" Mason asked warily.

"You'll see," Nora replied.

"Is it a treat to share? Is it something to eat?" Brody asked hopefully.

"No!"

She knew that people did eat ants in many parts of the world: Asia, South America, sub-Saharan Africa. There was no reason why the protein found in insects shouldn't be a food source for human beings as well as for other species. But she didn't want anybody eating *her* ants.

"Good morning, team," Coach Joe said in his usual hearty way. "Dunk, I'm not sure you're making the best choice about where to sit."

All week long, Dunk had plopped himself down next to Emma during the morning huddle and poked her with the eraser end of his pencil, yanked off her flowered headband, and threatened to remove his shoes so she'd have to smell his feet.

"So, Dunk, why don't you come over here and sit next to me?"

Scowling, Dunk obeyed.

"This morning, Nora has brought something fascinating to show to us. Something that has to do with science, because it's part of the natural world, but also has to do with social studies, because it can teach us a lot about how a colony needs to function. It even has to do with art, you might say, as what she's showing us is a pretty amazing work of art, too."

Coach Joe couldn't have given a better introduction if Nora had written it herself. It was a powerfully persuasive speech about the marvels of ants. And he had done a wonderful job of not revealing exactly what was still hidden under the T-shirt. He had left her the fun of revealing the final surprise.

"Nora," Coach Joe said, as her cue.

Nora smiled at her classmates. Mason and Brody would already know the surprise by now. They had both seen her ants at her house many times. So she focused her smiling on the other girls, especially Emma.

"What I have to show you," Nora said slowly, to prolong the suspense for one more sweet moment, "is . . ."

One last smile for good measure.

"My ant farm!"

She whisked off the T-shirt to reveal her scurrying ants in all their glory.

Emma shrieked. Not a giggling shriek this time, but a shriek of pure terror, horror, and loathing.

A few of the other girls joined in the screaming. Shrieking, it turned out, was contagious, a phenomenon some scientist should study sometime.

But Nora was not that scientist.

And now was not that time.

Emma fled from the huddle to the safety of her desk, as if the ants were loose instead of confined to an ant farm, and were painfully stinging ants instead of gentle ants from Nora's own backyard. Dunk dashed after Emma, pretending that he was

about to put an ant down the back of her pink-flowered top. Bethy followed as well, to try to get between Dunk and Emma, with Tamara and Elise trailing behind. Most of the other kids gathered around them, howling with laughter.

"Team!" Coach Joe bellowed. "Team, calm down!"

It did no good.

The only kids left in the huddle were three or four kids who also loved science, plus Amy, Mason, and Brody, Nora's most loyal friends.

Nora blinked back tears. She wasn't going to cry just because other people were totally ridiculous! But she felt—she tried to analyze what her emotions were right now—she felt *hurt*. Hurt on behalf of her ants. Hurt on behalf of science itself.

Coach Joe left his stool and stood facing the rest of the class.

"Team," he said somberly. "I have to say, you dropped the ball on this one. Nora, I'm sorry."

"That's okay," Nora said, covering up her ant farm with the T-shirt again.

Her classmates had made it clear: they hadn't yet been persuaded to like ants. But she'd be willing to bet that the editors of some famous, fancy science journal were soon going to let the world know that they liked her ants a *lot*.

Ants communicate in lots of different ways. One way is by using pheromones, which are chemical secretions they can taste and smell. Does Dunk think his smelly feet have pheromones to make Emma like him?

Nora refused to sit at her usual table that day at lunch. She took her sack lunch from home and headed outside to eat beneath the winter-bare trees. Kids were allowed to go outside for lunch recess whenever they were done in the cafeteria. Today, Nora was done from minute one.

Even though it was early January, the sun was so warm that she wasn't a bit chilly as she perched on the picnic table in her jacket and knit hat.

She was touched when Amy abandoned the other girls and came out to join her.

"If only Emma hadn't screamed," Amy said sorrowfully.

"I know."

"Sometimes I wish Emma weren't so . . . Emma-ish," Amy said.

"Me, too."

But Nora knew Emma was going to keep on being Emma-ish, just as she was going to keep on being Nora-ish. She wasn't really mad at Emma for screaming any more than she had been mad at her stinging ants for stinging. Both people and ants were what they were and did what they did. But if only people could be and do something different!

"Game tomorrow," Amy said, her voice more cheery. "We're playing the Killer Whales."

Dunk's team.

"Maybe we should change the name of our team," Amy suggested. "From the Fighting Bull-dogs to the Stinging Ants."

Nora laughed. She had told Amy the story about her first try at setting up an ant farm. "We'd be sure to win, then," she joked.

Besides, they had beaten Dunk's team once last fall. They could do it again tomorrow.

During the game the next morning, Nora didn't let herself think about ant experiments or cat videos. She focused her thoughts on positioning herself to shoot and on guarding one of Dunk's teammates, who was almost as big and beefy as Dunk himself.

At one point, as she was preparing to take a free throw after one Killer Whale had fouled her, she heard Dunk's taunt: "Ant lover!"

Apparently, Dunk thought that was an insult!

Nora showed him what a perfect shot an ant lover could make.

The Fighting Bulldogs, aka the Stinging Ants, won, 16–14.

At home that afternoon, Nora tried to think of the next experiment to do with her ants, the experiment that would make her name as a rising young scientist.

Was it cheating to ask her scientist parents for some ideas? Should a soon-to-be-famous scientist come up with breakthrough ideas all on her own, or was it all right to ask for help from other scientists?

Nora remembered a famous line said by one of the most famous scientists of all time: Sir Isaac Newton. One day, an apple fell on his head, and as he asked himself why it had fallen down rather than up, he discovered the law of gravity. So he had certainly had help from the apple. The famous line he had said was "If I have seen further (than others), it is by standing on the shoulders of giants." He didn't mean that he actually stood on the shoulders of tall people. He meant that his ideas had built on the ideas of the great scientists who had come before him.

Nora found her father at his extremely messy desk in his extremely messy upstairs office. That was another difference between her parents. Her father's desk was buried under stacks of paper piled every which way. Even the floor was barely visible, covered with a jumble of books, science journals, heaps of student final exams from last semester. Nora could hardly walk across the room without causing some pile of paper to topple. In contrast, her mother's office was as neat as could be, her desk

completely bare except for her laptop, a vase of flowers, and one coffee cup. Right now Nora could see that her father's desk had six or seven coffee cups on it—each one, she knew, half filled with coffee he had poured but forgotten to drink.

Nora was neat like her mother, not messy like her father. She liked her mother's office vastly better than she liked her father's office. But her father was the better parent to go to with a question about ants.

"Is it cheating if I ask you to help me come up

with an idea for the best ant farm experiment ever?" she asked.

There was no place to sit down in her dad's office—his couch was occupied with the same mess that spread over every other available surface. So she stood next to his desk while she waited for his answer to her question.

Her father thought for a while before replying. No matter what question she asked, he never answered right away.

"You'll still be the one doing the experiment," he finally said. "And interpreting the results. If you were to publish your findings"—*how did he know?!*—"it would be intellectually honest to have a footnote thanking anyone who helped you in your work. So you could say, 'I am grateful to Professor Neil Alpers for the suggestion to pursue this line of research.'"

Nora liked that wording. She could so easily imagine it in print.

"Can I have a piece of paper to write that down?" she asked.

"Sure. If there's one thing I have, it's pieces of paper. Finding a blank one, on the other hand, might not be so easy."

After some rummaging, he handed her a scrap of paper, somewhat stained from coffee, and a pencil. Nora scribbled down the words he had told her.

"So what *would* be a good line of research to pursue?" she asked.

He paused again to think. "You could take a few of the ants out of the farm," he said. "Put them in a measured area and see how long it takes them to find a piece of food placed outside the area. You'd be studying the ants in relation to both time and distance. You could keep increasing the distance of the food from their starting point. Is there some distance that is too far? Or will they keep seeking until they find what they are looking for?"

It was a perfect idea! Except for . . .

"Mom," Nora said. "She's not going to go in for taking the ants out of the ant farm. You know she's not."

"Good point." Another pause. "You can do it on one of her university days. Just make sure you put the experiment ants inside a larger enclosure so they don't get out. Like—the bathtub, maybe."

Nora didn't think her mother would like ants in the bathtub, either. But she'd use the bathtub in her own bathroom, not her parents' bathroom. Besides, science called for some sacrifices.

Just as Nora was measuring the dimensions of the bathtub, the phone rang. She was the only one in her family who ever answered the phone, as both of her parents got all their important calls on their cell phones and Nora didn't have a cell phone yet.

"Hello?"

"Nora, can you come over? Right away?"

It was Mason, sounding more upset than she had ever heard him before.

"What happened? Is it Dog? Is Dog okay?"

"Dog's been skunked!"

Ants can leave lots of different messages with their pheromones. They can warn other ants about danger. They can tell other ants where to find food. Thing to find out: does skunk spray contain pheromones?

Although the afternoon had been as unseasonably warm as the rest of the week, darkness was falling and the night air was frosty as Nora hurried to Mason's house, a few blocks away. She could smell the pungent odor of skunk, stronger than her father's strongest coffee, as soon as she turned the corner onto Mason's street. How could one small animal produce such an enormous stink? What was that smelly stuff *made* of? What chemicals combined to make a stink so horrific?

By the time she reached Mason's house, which

was right next door to Brody's house, Nora's eyes were stinging and her nose was crinkling. She could see the boys outside, crouched next to Dog in the pool of bright light from the light fixture over the garage door.

It was one of the saddest sights she had ever seen.

Mason was trying to get Dog not to rub the spray from his face with his paws, as Brody sat next to him with streaming eyes—whether from the skunk smell or from tears, Nora couldn't tell.

"Don't, Dog," Mason pleaded. "You'll just make it worse."

"Where are your parents?" Nora asked.

"They're out on a date night with Brody's parents," Mason said. "Cammie and Cara are 'babysitting.'"

Cammie and Cara were Brody's older sisters, who were nowhere in sight.

"They're inside," Brody explained, "trying to call my parents or Mason's parents to find out what to do."

"What we need to do," Nora said, "is wash Dog. Now."

"In the bathtub?" Mason asked.

Nora could tell he was wondering if his mother would really want Dog inside the house, dragged all the way up the carpeted staircase to the upstairs bathroom. A skunked dog would be a worse thing to find in your bathtub than a few little ants.

"No. We don't need to wash all of him. In fact, we don't *want* to wash all of him. We don't want to get the stinky stuff on his front half all over the fur that doesn't stink yet, or then all of him will stink."

"What do we wash him with?" Brody asked.

"Hydrogen peroxide."

"Whatever that is," Mason said. "Which we probably don't have. And can't get, because none of us can drive anywhere to get it."

Cammie and Cara came back outside. They were both in middle school and even more giggly than Emma herself. But neither one was giggling now.

"They're not answering their phones!" Cammie wailed. "They went to some dumb classical music concert and turned their phones off!"

"They don't even care that we're here all by ourselves trying to figure out what to do with the world's stinkiest dog!" Cara moaned.

"Do you have any hydrogen peroxide?" Nora interrupted.

Brody's sisters stopped their wailing and moaning, and gave Nora a look of utter confusion.

"Yes," Cammie said. "I use it to put highlights in my hair. You want some *now*? Anyway, that kind of highlight will look strange in dark hair like yours. It'll make you look—"

"Like a skunk," Cara finished the sentence.

Nora rolled her eyes. "Hydrogen peroxide," she explained, "helps neutralize the smell from a skunk."

"Oh!" Cammie started to race inside Brody's house to get it.

"There's other stuff we need, too," Nora called after her. Cammie waited to hear the rest. "Baking soda? I think we need baking soda. And a bucket of water. And a sponge, of course, to wash him. But first we need to look up how much hydrogen peroxide we need and how much baking soda, and if there's any other ingredients to add."

Cara was already searching for it on her phone. "A bottle of hydrogen peroxide. I think we have almost a full bottle. And a quarter cup of baking soda. I know my mom has some baking soda somewhere. And we need some dish detergent. And some warm water, too."

The sisters headed back inside together, on a mission now.

"It's my fault," Brody said, in a small voice, as Dog lay whimpering beside him. "I'm the one who wanted to take him for one more walk, because it was such a nice day. He pulled away before I could get the leash on and ran after something. I thought it was a squirrel or a rabbit, and I yelled at him to stop. But . . ."

He didn't need to finish the sentence.

Nora pulled off her hat and held it over her nose to block out some of the smell. Her eyes still stung.

"Poor Dog," she said. "How could Dog get skunked in *January*? I thought skunks weren't very active in the winter. I read that in a library book over winter break."

"I guess this skunk can't read," Mason muttered.

Maybe the warmer weather this past week had made the skunk think it was spring. But spring in January appeared to be over. A gust of bitter wind made Nora shiver.

Cammie and Cara reappeared with the ingredients for Dog's de-skunking bath and the bucket to mix them in.

Nora took charge of the mixing. It was like an experiment with her chemistry set. The peroxide made the liquid in the bucket fizzle.

"Okay," she said. "It's ready."

"Here, Dog," Mason said gently. "Brody and I are going to make that awful smell go away."

He dipped a sponge into the peroxide mixture and started wiping Dog's face and shoulders. Brody took a second sponge and wiped Dog from the other side.

Dog whimpered again. He looked better now, without any of that oozy gunk on him. Nora couldn't tell if he smelled better or not. The smell of skunk was so powerful that it wasn't going to go away immediately, no matter how much hydrogen peroxide was rubbed on Dog.

Feebly, Dog licked Mason's hand, and then licked Brody's. He seemed to know that his two masters were trying to help.

"I'm sorry, Dog," Brody whispered, as if he had been the one who had suggested to Dog that it

would be a good idea to dash off after some strange black-and-white-striped animal.

Headlights appeared down the road, and Brody's parents' car pulled into the driveway, squealing to a stop.

"We tried to call!" Mason's mother said, leaping out of the backseat.

"*We* tried to call!" Mason shot back.

"Well, we got your message, and we're here now."

"It's good you washed him right away," Mason's dad said. "What are you washing him with?"

"Hydrogen peroxide, baking soda, some liquid detergent, and warm water," Brody replied.

"How on earth did you know what to do?" his mother asked.

"Nora told us," Brody said.

"Nora!" all the parents exclaimed in unison.

Nora stood, uncomfortable, as the parents continued to heap praise upon her. "I'm so glad the boys thought to call you!" "Talk about a quick mind in a crisis!" "I never would have thought of hydrogen peroxide!" "We're so lucky you were here!" If they were this impressed that she happened to remember one simple fact about hydrogen peroxide, what would they do when they read her published article about ants?

"Now, Mason," Mason's mother said, "even after this washing, he's still going to smell for a while. You know that, don't you?"

Mason looked puzzled. "What if he does?"

Mason's mother made her voice firm: "Dog needs to sleep in the garage tonight. I can't have him smelling up the entire house."

"No!" Mason and Brody cried together.

"It's cold in the garage!" Mason said.

"It's not even going to reach freezing tonight, and Dog has a nice warm fur coat," Mrs. Dixon pointed out.

"He'll think he's being punished," Brody said. "He'll think he did something wrong."

"Running after a skunk isn't the best or smartest thing he's ever done," Mason's father put in.

"Mom, he doesn't smell *that* bad," Mason insisted. "After a while, you get used to it."

"I have no intention of getting used to that smell in my house."

This time, both boys seemed to know they were defeated.

Then Brody's face brightened. It never took too long for Brody's face to brighten.

"Can we sleep in the garage, too?" he asked.

Even Mason's face brightened. And it took a lot to make Mason's face brighten. "So he'll know we still love him?" he joined in the pleading.

The four parents exchanged glances. The two sisters exchanged giggles.

"They do have sleeping bags," Mason's mom said slowly.

"And they can come inside if they get too cold," Brody's mom added.

"Hooray!" Brody said. "Dog, we're going to have a sleepover all night in the garage! You and Mason and me. And Nora! Nora, can you come, too?"

Nora hesitated. She was fond of Mason. She was fond of Brody. She was fond of Dog. But friendship had its limits.

"I think Nora has too much sense to want to sleep on a hard cement floor next to a stinking dog in an unheated garage in the middle of January," Mrs. Dixon said. "Am I correct, Nora?"

"I do need to get home," Nora said, trying to sound more reluctant than she actually felt.

Right this minute she was extra-glad that she had pets that didn't chase after skunks and get themselves banished to spending the night outside.

She took one last look at Brody and Mason. Both boys had laid their heads against Dog's broad back, one on each side, apparently not minding his dampness and smell.

Then she walked home under the golden street-lights to spend a cozy, warm evening indoors with her ants.

Ants also communicate by sound—they make tiny little squeaks. And they tap and stroke each other, too. I can't hear my ants squeaking. Can they hear me?

"So let's talk about persuasive speeches," Coach Joe said in the Monday-morning huddle. "What's the point of a persuasive speech?"

Nora hated when teachers asked questions that had super-obvious answers. She would feel silly raising her hand and saying, "The point of a persuasive speech is to try to persuade somebody of something so that they end up persuaded."

Emma never minded stating the obvious. "To persuade somebody," she said.

"Great!"

Emma gave a simpering little smile at Coach Joe's recognition of her brilliance.

"So what does that mean?" This time, fortunately, Coach Joe answered his own question. "It means that the person you're trying to persuade isn't yet persuaded, right? So what you're really trying to do in a persuasive speech is to change someone's mind. The audience for your speech is someone who isn't already rooting for your team. You want to make new fans, not play to the same fans you've had all season."

"You're never going to change some people's minds," Mason said. If Emma was the master of stating the obvious, Mason was the master of stating the negative.

"True," Coach Joe said. "You're completely right, Mason. Some people are just never going to be convinced by any challenge to what they already think. Patrick Henry and Thomas Paine, two of the best persuasive-speech writers of the American Revolution, knew they were never going to convince King George the Third or die-hard British loyalists. So who were they trying to convince?"

Nora raised her hand this time. "People who

hadn't made up their minds yet. People who were torn between both sides."

"Exactly. So maybe I misspoke earlier. The goal isn't so much to change someone's mind; that can be pretty tough, as our friend Mason pointed out. The goal of a persuasive speech is to help someone make up her mind. But that means speaking to the part of her mind that is tempted to favor the other side."

Some of the kids in the huddle had tuned out. Emma was fiddling with her charm bracelet, a silver chain hung with lots of little silver cats in different poses. Dunk, still made to sit right next to Coach Joe, appeared to be sleeping. Dunk's idea of persuading somebody would be threatening to sic his awful dog, Wolf, on them if they didn't give in.

"So," Coach Joe said, clearly realizing that he was losing half his team, "step one in writing a persuasive speech is figuring out your subject. But step two is equally important: figuring out your audience. Huddle dismissed. Back to your seats. You can talk quietly to your pod mates about your ideas. Just remember to ask: Who would be disagreeing with me? And why?"

Nora sat in a six-desk pod this month with Brody, Emma, and three other boys she didn't know very well. Coach Joe liked to move kids around. He called it changing the lineup. Poor Mason and Amy were currently in a pod with Dunk.

"So what do you want to write your persuasive speech about?" Nora asked. Someone needed to take charge of pod discussions, and that someone usually turned out to be her. At least it was easier to lead a discussion than it was to de-skunk a dog.

"I don't know," Jack said.

"I don't know," Nahil said.

"I don't know," Austin said.

Or maybe de-skunking a dog was easier.

"I know what I'm going to write about," Brody volunteered. "Mine is going to be great! It's going to be terrific! If people had only heard my speech in 1775, the whole course of history would have been different!"

Nora knew Brody well enough to know that he wasn't really bragging, however braggy he sounded. It was just his way of being enthusiastic. It wasn't bragging if Dog wagged his tail so hard it practically knocked someone over.

"Do you want to know what I'm going to write about?" Brody asked the others.

"No," Jack, Nahil, and Austin said in unison.

"Sure," Nora and Emma said at the same time.

Brody evidently preferred to listen to Nora and Emma.

"I'm going to persuade the colonists and the British *not* to have a war! To work out their differences in a peaceful way! If the British would just lower taxes and not tax things the colonists really love, like tea, the colonists wouldn't want to revolt, and the British could keep their colonies and get at least *some* tax money from them, which is better than none. Right? And nobody would die, which is even better. Right? And today we'd all be singing 'God Save the Queen' *and* 'My Country, 'Tis of Thee,' which would be perfect, because they both have the same tune anyway."

Brody's face was lit up with excitement. Nora could tell that he was ready to write his acceptance speech for the Nobel Peace Prize.

"I like it," Emma said.

Emma usually liked anything any boy wanted her to like, unless it was a boy she *really* liked, such as Dunk, and then she had to make a big show of pretending to hate it.

Brody's eyes sparkled from Emma's praise. Nora could tell he was waiting for her to praise him, too.

"Well," she said slowly, "preventing war is definitely a good thing to do. But don't you think the colonists already tried to make persuasive speeches to get their demands met? They didn't start out planning to go to war. War was their last resort, wasn't it?"

"Of course they tried," Brody agreed. "But I'm going to try harder. I'm going to try better."

"What are *you* going to write about?" Nora asked Emma.

"I'm going to write about"—Emma had raised her voice, clearly so that the people in the next pod would be able to hear her—"how cats are better than dogs."

Dunk got up from his pod and walked over to theirs.

"Oh yeah?" he said.

Emma giggled.

Dunk leaned in closer. "Well, I just decided what *I'm* going to write about."

Nora could tell that Dunk was relieved to have any idea at all.

"I'm going to write about how dogs are better than cats."

Emma giggled again.

"Dunk, back to your seat," Coach Joe called out.

"What do you think of my idea?" Emma asked her pod mates once Dunk had stomped away.

Jack, Nahil, and Austin shrugged.

"The problem with it is," Brody said, "that cats aren't better than dogs. Dunk is right." Certainly, this was the first time Brody had ever given Dunk credit for being right about anything. "My dog is the best animal in the whole world. No, in the whole universe."

"Nora, what do you think?" Emma asked, obviously hoping that the girls could stick together.

Nora copied her father and thought for a moment before answering.

"Actually, I don't think dogs are better *or* cats are better. Or pigs or porcupines. Animals aren't better or worse. They just are. That's like asking, 'Which are better, girls or boys?'"

"Girls!" Emma said, just as Jack, Nahil, and Austin said, "Boys!"

Brody didn't cast a vote on that one. He evidently didn't feel as strongly about boys versus girls as he did about dogs versus cats.

Nora shook her head. She should have realized that was a bad example.

"Anyway," she said, "it's good that our pod has a dog person and a cat person. It's like what Coach

Joe said. You have to try to persuade people who don't already agree with you. So Emma can try to persuade Brody."

Except that would be impossible.

"What about you, Nora?" Brody asked. "What are you going to write about?"

How ants are better than anything?

How people, such as Emma, should know more about science?

How there should be more famous women scientists, like Marie Curie? And, soon, Nora Alpers?

"I don't know," Nora admitted.

And then she realized that she sounded exactly like Jack, Nahil, and Austin.

Ants have been around for a long, long time. Scientists have found ant fossils in Europe that are more than 90 million years old. I hope they will be around for 90 million more years, at least.

After school on Monday, Nora went over to Mason's house to visit Dog and see how he was recovering from his encounter with the skunk.

"He doesn't smell at all anymore," Brody assured her as the three of them walked the few blocks to Mason's house. Mason's mom worked at home, editing an online knitting newsletter, so she was always there to welcome Mason and his friends.

"Well, he still smells a little bit," Mason corrected. "My parents looked it up on the Internet, and it's going to take a while for the skunk smell to go away completely."

"Like how long?" Nora asked.

"A couple of months," Mason admitted.

"So not very long at all!" Brody added.

When Dog ran up to greet them, tail wagging, Nora thought he smelled a *lot*.

"I know," Mason's mom said, in response to Nora's involuntarily wrinkled nose. "But I can't make him sleep in the garage forever. The three of you must be hungry. How about some roasted red pepper hummus and pita bread?"

"Hummus and pita sounds lovely," Nora said politely, even though she wasn't sure about the roasted red pepper part.

Brody, who liked all foods, nodded in happy agreement.

Mason had already gone to the pantry and grabbed a bag of Fig Newtons. Mason liked to eat the same foods over and over again: macaroni and cheese (from a box), peanut butter and jelly sandwiches, Cheerios (plain), and Fig Newtons (the original figgy kind).

"Fig Newtons, anyone?" he offered.

"Mason," his mother said, watching him put two Fig Newtons on a small plate and pour himself a glass of milk. "How do you know you aren't going to like hummus if you've never even tried it?"

"I don't have to try it to know it isn't Fig Newtons," Mason replied. "I don't have to try—what was that thing you tried to make me eat the other day? Baba something—baba smoosh?"

"Baba ghanoush," his mother said. "A delicious Middle Eastern dish of mashed eggplant and tahini."

"Baba whatever," Mason said. "I rest my case. I don't have to try mashed eggplant to know that it isn't macaroni and cheese. Even the word *eggplant* gives me the creeps. Doesn't it give you the creeps?" he asked Nora and Brody.

"Well, no," Nora said, even though she hated to side against Mason. Words weren't creepy; they were just words. Besides, lots of people thought things were creepy, like worms, spiders, snakes, and even ants, just because they didn't know anything about them. Mason's mother was right. Mason should give hummus and baba ghanoush a chance.

"Eggplant sounds like a plant that has eggs growing on it," Brody said. "That's weird, but not creepy weird, just funny weird."

"Mason," his mother said sadly, "what do I have to do to persuade you to at least *try* something new?"

Mason gave no reply. He just took another bite of Fig Newton.

Aside from smelling like burnt rubber, Dog was his old self, eager to go outside and dash after the battered tennis ball they threw for him in the yard. Even if he would never break any Guinness World Records for tennis ball fetching, he darted after the ball as quickly as if he were a dog with four legs.

"Guess what my mom is trying to make me do once basketball ends?" Mason asked. By his tone, Nora could tell he thought it was something extremely terrible.

"Voice lessons," Nora guessed. The music teacher at Plainfield Elementary was always telling Mason what a lovely voice he had, and Nora knew Mason lived in dread of being made to take voice lessons.

Mason shook his head.

"Joining some club that has Dunk in it?" Brody asked.

Nora tried to think of a club Dunk would join. She couldn't.

"No," Mason told them. "You'll never guess. No one could ever guess. So I'll have to tell you. My mother is trying to talk me into . . ."

He paused for effect.

"Figure skating! Ice skating! Doing fancy twirls and leaps and stuff on the ice!"

Nora couldn't help it. She burst out laughing. Brody doubled over, laughing, too.

Dog came up, panting, a ball in his mouth.

"At least Dog doesn't think it's funny," Mason said.

But Dog did look as if he were grinning as he dropped the ball at Mason's feet.

"If only," Mason said, "I could find a way to persuade my parents to stop trying to persuade *me* to do things!"

Monday evening, Nora's mother was off listening to an astronomy talk at the university, so Nora and her father were home all by themselves. All by themselves, except for her ants.

"I'm going to work on my ant experiments," Nora told her father as they cleared away the dishes after dinner.

"Do you need any help?" he asked.

"No!" Nora hadn't meant to sound so fierce, but it was one thing to have a footnote thanking Professor Neil Alpers for suggesting her line of research. It would be quite another thing if she had to thank Prof. Neil Alpers for helping with the research itself.

"Okay, sweetie" was all her father said. "If you need me, you know where to find me."

Nora had already cut a large sheet from a huge roll of butcher paper stored in the attic. She thought her ants would be more comfortable walking across paper than across the slippery, cold, bare bathtub. Now she laid the paper in the bottom of the tub, measured a square in the middle of it, and marked the square with bright blue chalk.

Gently, she extricated a dozen ants from her farm. Those would be enough ants to start with. She placed them in the middle of the square and set a small piece of cracker outside the square. Then she set the stopwatch on the tablet she had borrowed from her father.

The ants walked about. In two minutes and twenty-three seconds, the first ant reached the chalk line on one edge of the square, the edge farthest from the cracker.

Then the ant stopped.

Another ant followed her. (Nora knew they were

both female ants, because all worker ants are females.)

That ant stopped, too.

Nora stared. Ants didn't seem to want to cross
a line made of chalk! How could they even know
there was a line there? Why would they care? They
must have smelled the chalk or felt the chalk dust
with their feet.

As Nora continued to watch, two other ants
stopped short their wanderings at a different edge
of the square, also reluctant to walk across the
chalk line.

She drew in her breath. This was a pattern! This
was a real, observable, scientific result!

But three other ants, which had reached the
edge of the chalk square closest to the cracker,
hesitated, and then did cross over the line, taking
a direct path to the cracker.

Ants were willing to cross the chalk line if there
was food on the other side!

Wishing she had remembered to bring her parents' video camera up to the bathroom, Nora con-
tented herself with watching and timing. Sir Isaac
Newton hadn't had a video camera to record the
falling apple. He had just watched it fall.

For the next hour, Nora sat on the rim of the bathtub, completely still, blissfully watching, measuring, and timing her ants.

There are about 12,500 species of ants known to science. Maybe I will discover some new ant species someday. I think I already made a huge, important ant discovery today!

On Tuesday, Emma wore a pink sweater with a fluffy white cat on it to school. The cat wasn't flat; it poofed out of the sweater with soft, fuzzy white yarn. An actual small plaid ribbon perched on top of its head.

The girls at lunch squealed with rapture.

"It looks so real!" Bethy said. "Can I pat its fur?"

"If your hands are clean," Emma told her. "Not if you've been eating."

"I haven't even touched my tuna melt yet," Bethy promised.

With one gentle finger, she stroked the fur of Emma's sweater cat.

"It's so soft!" she exclaimed.

"Can I touch it?" Elise asked.

"Me, too!" chimed in Tamara. Even Amy gave the sweater an admiring smile.

Nora made sure to take a first bite of her tuna melt sandwich so that her hands wouldn't meet Emma's cat-petting standard.

"Sorry," she mumbled, with her mouth full. "I was starving!"

"It's soooo cute," Amy admitted. "Her ribbon even has sparkles on it."

"Mega-cute," Elise agreed. "Look! She has real whiskers!"

"The cutest cat in the world!" Tamara gushed.

The sudden frosty look on Emma's face let Tamara know that her praise of the sweater cat had gone too far.

"Except for Precious Cupcake, of course," Tamara hastily corrected herself. "Precious Cupcake is the cutest *real* cat in the world. This is the cutest *cat on a sweater* in the world."

Emma's smile returned.

"I know," she said.

Nora chomped down on another bite of tuna melt. She wouldn't have minded all the fuss over Emma's cat sweater if she hadn't known how differently the girls—well, except for Amy—would have reacted if she had worn a pink sweater covered with little black ants.

"Ewww!"

"Gross!"

"They look so real!"

Screams from Emma. A stampede away from the table.

Maybe Nora should defy the code of the Plainfield Elementary animal kingdom and go sit with Mason and Brody and their other friends. But she knew she wouldn't; she couldn't. Animal kingdom behavior wasn't that easy to change, even if a human animal really wanted to change it.

Nora took a big swig of milk to force down a bite of sandwich she was having trouble swallowing.

On Wednesday, Dunk wore a T-shirt that said I HATE CATS. Beneath the slogan was a big red circle crossing out the silhouette of a cat. The T-shirt looked brand-new, unlike Dunk's usual clothes, which bore stubborn stains of catsup, mustard, and whatever his horrid dog, Wolf, had rolled in lately.

As soon as Dunk yanked off his jacket in the cubby room, Emma's eyes widened.

"Ooh!" she seethed, jabbing him in the chest. Her rage today seemed real to Nora rather than pretend. You could sound mad even if you weren't really angry. It would be a lot harder to make your cheeks flush on demand.

Dunk grinned.

Other boys whooped and hollered and thumped him on the back.

Emma's friends formed a protective circle around her as Nora stood watching. Nora had no interest in taking sides in the war between cat lovers and dog lovers in Coach Joe's class. But if she were to take sides, right now she'd side with Emma. It was one thing to love your own kind of pet. It was another to hate someone else's kind of pet.

When Dunk tried to sit next to Emma in Coach Joe's huddle, even before Coach Joe could make Dunk move, Emma got up and flounced away.

Dunk gave his usual donkey-like guffaw.

He plainly didn't get the difference between Emma's fake rage and her real rage.

But Nora did.

After school, Nora hung out with Amy. The two girls went for a walk with Amy's two dogs, Nora walking Amy's big dog, Woofer, on one leash while Amy walked her little dog, Tweeter, on another. It was considerate of Amy to have a dog for each of them.

Amy had a cat for each friend, too. Earlier in the afternoon, Mush Ball had been cuddling on Nora's lap while Snookers had been snuggling with Amy.

Amy even had a rabbit for each of them out in a hutch in her backyard, and a pair of parakeets in a cage in her dining room.

But there was one pet Amy didn't have, the best pet of all: ants.

"So which do *you* think is better, dogs or cats?" Nora asked, knowing which answer she hoped Amy would give.

"Neither! I mean, why do we have to take sides? Dogs are better at being dogs, and cats are better at being cats."

Nora couldn't have said it better herself.

Woofer stopped to smell something buried under the new snow. Nora had read that a dog's sense of smell was thousands of times better than a human's. Even though a dog brain was only one-tenth the size of a human brain, the smelling part of its brain was forty times larger.

For a moment, Nora envied Amy for having so many different animals she could study, so many notebooks' worth of fascinating facts. But maybe it was better to study one subject in greater depth. Her mother was an expert on Saturn, not Saturn *and* Jupiter *and* Mars. It was enough to be an expert on Saturn—and not even on all of Saturn, just on its rings.

As they walked on, Amy said, "I thought I'd write my persuasive speech about how people shouldn't dress up their pets in costumes. Pets hate costumes! And it's almost like we're making fun of them, laughing at how ridiculous they look. You know what I mean?"

Nora certainly did.

"But then I thought . . . well, you know . . ."

"Emma," Nora said.

"She wouldn't like it."

That was an understatement.

"But I feel sorry for Precious Cupcake sometimes, I really do," Amy said.

"Me, too," Nora said.

Woofer stopped to sniff at a tree. Tweeter strained at his leash to dart after a squirrel. And then the two girls walked on.

That evening, Nora worked on writing her ant article. She thought of a catchy title for it: "The Ants Go Marching—Until They Reach the Chalk Line!" Maybe the editors would think that was an attention-getting title. She would certainly want to read an article with that title.

She had repeated the same experiment three times on Monday night and gotten the same results. That was important in science. You didn't know if your results were real, and not just a fluke, unless you got the same results over and over again. So she put that in her article, too. And she made a chart of all her measurements: how long it had taken the ants to reach the perimeter of the square, how long it had taken them to cross the chalk line to reach the cracker.

This was going to be the best ant article ever!

In school on Thursday, Dunk wore his I HATE CATS T-shirt again, apparently not noticing that it hadn't gotten the results he wanted on Wednesday. Nora was struck by how much more quickly her ants were willing to change their behavior when a strategy wasn't working.

Emma wasn't wearing her fuzzy-cat sweater, but she had on her cat necklace *and* a cat charm bracelet. She spent most of the day, as far as Nora could tell, fiddling with them. Lunchtime was non-stop cat videos. The other girls seemed a bit worn out with gushing.

"I think we saw that one already," Amy said.

"My mother said I could have an ice-skating party for my birthday," Tamara said, daring to change the subject.

Nora couldn't help wondering if Mason's mother had signed him up for ice-skating lessons yet.

"I love ice skating!" Elise said.

"Me, too!" said Bethy.

"Speaking of ice skating, I have a video of Precious Cupcake outside in the snow," Emma said. "Let me see if I can find it."

But the other girls just kept on talking about how much fun an ice-skating party would be, especially if they could wear special ice-skating skirts and send invitations cut out in the shape of ice skates.

At home that afternoon, Nora sat down at the computer in the family room to try to type her ant article. A real science journal would expect articles to be typed, not written out by hand. She didn't have a computer of her own, but her parents let her use the computer and printer on the desk in the family room whenever she wanted. Luckily, her mother made her father keep all of his mess contained in his own office, so the family room desk was always an invitingly neat place for Nora to work.

If only she were a faster typist. Coach Joe's class went to the computer lab twice a week for keyboarding, but Nora still typed so slowly and made so many mistakes. When she heard her parents typing, their fingers flew over the keys with amazing speed, especially her father's. He could probably be in the *Guinness World Records* book for fastest typing.

Sitting at the computer, Nora created a new file—*Nora ant article*—and typed in her first sentence: "Is there aynthing in the wrld more fscinatnig than ants?"

Coach Joe liked them to begin with a question to engage the reader. She hoped the editors of a grown-up science journal would like the same thing.

Reading her sentence over, she saw four mistakes in it. It took her another two minutes to correct them: "Is there anything in the world more fascinating than ants?"

Maybe she could ask her father to type the article for her. It wasn't very long. He could probably type it in five minutes. It would take her more like five hours. No, not five hours. Nora wasn't one for dramatic exaggeration. But it would take her a frustrating amount of time. It wouldn't be cheating if he typed it for her so long as she added that to her thank-you footnote:

"I would like to thank Professor Neil Alpers for suggesting this line of research and for typing this article for me."

She saved her one completed sentence on the computer—she certainly didn't want to have to type the whole thing over again—and wandered up to her dad's messy office. She hadn't told either of her parents yet about her publication plan. The thought of telling them made her feel shy for some reason. They had always supported her love of science. How could they not, given that they were both scientists themselves? But they might say, "Oh, honey, I don't think a real grown-up journal is going to want an ant article by a ten-year-old."

Would a real grown-up science journal want an ant article by a ten-year-old?

Nora felt a twinge of doubt.

Maybe her first sentence didn't sound scientific enough. Coach Joe's advice might not apply to scientific articles; maybe those articles weren't supposed to begin with a question. Their readers were probably already so wild to learn about science that they wanted to jump right in and skip the beginning stuff altogether.

And she didn't even know of any ant journals where she could send her article. How would she know which ant journals were the best?

Her father was hunched over his computer, typing at his usual Guinness World Record speed.

"What's up?" he asked, swirling toward her in his big swivel chair.

"Nothing." She moved a pile of journals from his couch to the floor so that she could sit down, careful to keep them all in order. Her father claimed that even though his office looked like a mess, he knew exactly where everything was.

The top journal in the pile was called *Nature*.

Nature was a huge subject. It would include every single thing in the natural world. Including ants.

Nora picked it up and thumbed through it. She saw lots of graphs. She'd have to be sure to put graphs in her article. Luckily, she already knew how to make graphs on the computer. There were lots of footnotes, too, numbered stuff in little type at the bottom of each page. At least she'd have one footnote, the thank-you to Professor Alpers. One footnote was better than nothing.

"Did you ever have an article in this one?" she asked her dad.

"Once. That's a tough one to get in, because it has so many different kinds of science in it."

"How did they know to pick you? Did they already know how smart you are?"

He chuckled. "Hardly. They send each article off to experts in the field. The experts review it blind. That means without knowing who wrote it, so they won't be influenced by anything except by how good the science is."

Nora liked that part. The ant experts who read her article wouldn't know that she was only ten. They would just care about how much she knew about ants.

"So anybody could publish an article here if it was good enough?" she persisted.

Her father nodded.

"Even a kid?"

To her great disappointment, he didn't give her an encouraging grin.

"Well . . ."

"Why not a kid?" Nora demanded.

"Well, there's no reason why a person's age in

itself should make a difference," he said slowly. "But I have to say, it's exceedingly unlikely that a child would be able to compete against adult scientists with their doctorate degrees and fancy labs."

Nora lifted her chin.

Did any of those adult scientists, with their doctorate degrees and fancy labs, love ants the way she did?

And that girl in the record book, Emily Rosa: she hadn't had a doctorate degree or a fancy lab, and she was only a year older than Nora.

"Is there anything you came in to ask me?" her father asked, glancing over at his computer screen as if he wanted to get back to work.

"No," Nora said. "Can I borrow this?" She held up the copy of *Nature.*

"Sure."

Nora thought he looked amused. Had he figured out that she was planning to send her ant article off to *Nature* as soon as she finished typing it? Now she was definitely going to type it all by herself, without help from any grown-up. She was never going to ask for help from a grown-up on anything ever again!

Did her father think she was *funny*?

Even worse, did he think she was *cute*?

Without another word, Nora stalked out of his office and shut the door.

Let her father try to hide a smile! She was going to show Professor Neil Alpers just what a ten-year-old ant-loving scientist could do.

Ants differ enormously in size. An entire colony of the smallest ants could fit inside the head of one of the most giant ants! But just because some ants are smaller, that doesn't make them any less important.

10

It took Nora two hours to type her article. When she printed it out, it was only four pages, including the graphs, which were in color.

Was that too short for a real grown-up article?

No, she decided. What mattered in science were your experiment and what it proved: your data. You didn't need to go on and on about it for pages, just repeating the same points over and over.

She looked again at her graphs.

Ants busy in their tunnels were the most beautiful thing in the world. But the second-most beautiful thing was graphs about ants, printed in color!

She probably needed to write a letter to go with the article. The letter didn't have to be long, either. This was a business letter, not a friendly letter, so she used the format Coach Joe had taught them for business letters. She was too worn out from typing the article to type the letter, too. But she wrote it in cursive, even though she wasn't very good at cursive. Cursive looked more grown-up and business-like than printing.

Dear Sir or Madam:
    Here is the article I wrote about my research into ants.
        I hope you want to publish it.
                Sincerely,
                Nora Alpers

She found an envelope in the desk drawer and wrote the address on it. Her parents kept a roll of stamps in the drawer, too. They were both great believers in writing old-fashioned letters, the kind you wrote by hand and sent in the mail, so they had told her she could help herself to stamps whenever she needed one.

"I'm going for a walk!" she called upstairs to them.

Faintly, her mother's voice called back, "Dinner in half an hour!"

The closest mailbox was in front of the post office, just three blocks away, in the other direction from where Amy lived. Nora could have put her letter for pickup in the mailbox at home, but then her parents might see it. She wasn't going to tell them anything until the issue with the published article came in the mail. Even then she wasn't going to *tell* them. She'd let them find out on their own.

The new issue would arrive in the mail.

Her father would flip through it before sticking it on the top of one of the huge piles of paper in his office.

His eyes would fall on a familiar name.

He'd stare at it, unable to believe what he saw.

"Nora!" he'd holler. "Nora, is this *you*? Janine, come see what our daughter just did!"

These pleasant thoughts occupied Nora all the way to the post office. Now she stood in front of the mailbox, her letter clutched tightly in her hand.

She wasn't a superstitious person. She didn't believe in magic or luck or special charms to make things happen. But she still gave her envelope one little kiss—not for luck, really, just to wish it success on its way.

She slipped it into the mail slot and hugged herself with happiness.

At lunch on Friday, Emma started talking as soon as all the girls had sat down. She always talked more than everybody else put together, but today she obviously had something extra-important to share.

"Over winter break, my mother took me and my sister to the Brown Palace Hotel in Denver for high tea. *High tea* means extra-fancy tea. You don't just have tea; you also have scones—these yummy little biscuit things—with cream and jam. And itty-bitty cucumber sandwiches—I know that sounds weird, but they're ultra-British, and they're good, too. They really are, with the crusts cut off to make them even fancier. Plus lots of little frosted cakes. And everyone was all dressed up—with hats! And a lady wearing a long dress was playing beautiful music on a harp. It was the best time I ever had in my life."

Nora was surprised that the best time Emma ever had in her life was a time Precious Cupcake hadn't even been there.

"There was one thing missing, of course," Emma said then.

Of course.

"Precious Cupcake couldn't come with me, because they don't allow pets at their high tea. *Any* pets. So . . ."

Emma paused. When all eyes were on her, she continued.

"I'm going to have my own high tea just for Precious Cupcake and a few of my best friends. It's going to be this Sunday afternoon from three to five. I know this is short notice, but can you all come? Say yes!"

"Yes!" chorused Bethy, Elise, Tamara, and Amy. A high tea like the one at the Brown Palace Hotel was even more exciting than an ice-skating party.

"Nora, you're invited, too," Emma said, as if Nora might be hesitating because she wasn't sure if she was a best-enough best friend to be included in such a select invitation.

Nora didn't particularly want to eat cucumber sandwiches with Emma's cat. But she didn't want to hurt Emma's feelings, either, especially since Dunk was wearing his now grubby and stained I HATE CATS T-shirt for the third day in a row. Emma, who usually never wore the same outfit twice in a month, was wearing her fluffy-cat sweater for the second time that week.

"Thank you," Nora said. "I'd love to."

Coach Joe let kids bring in treats on their birthdays. Today was the birthday of one of Brody's friends, Sheng. So Sheng's mother had brought in cupcakes.

When the school day was almost over, Sheng went around setting paper plates with cupcakes on them on everybody's desks.

Emma beamed as if Sheng had chosen to bring cupcakes in honor of Precious Cupcake. "Thank you," she told him, with the kind of smile she used to give to Dunk. "I love cupcakes."

She turned toward Nora. "We'll be having mini-cupcakes at the high tea in addition to the scones and cucumber sandwiches. Of course!"

"That will be nice," Nora said politely.

"Cupcakes are awesome," Brody agreed, his face already dabbed with frosting.

Out of the corner of her eye, Nora saw Dunk heading toward their pod.

Emma had been snubbing Dunk all week. No

giggles when he told her that Wolf could eat Precious Cupcake for breakfast. No girly squeals when he jostled her tray in the lunch line and slopped tomato soup all over her grilled cheese sandwich. No one could do frosty disdain better than Emma Averill, Nora had to give her that.

But Dunk still didn't seem to get it. The more Emma snubbed him, the harder he tried to impress her by horsing around with the other boys and saying mean things about cats in general and Precious Cupcake in particular.

Now he approached, cupcake in hand.

"*Precious Cupcake* is a dumb name for a cat," Dunk said, as a friendly opening.

Nora couldn't disagree with that.

He grinned at Emma hopefully, plainly expecting that she would finally break down and giggle again as in days of yore.

She didn't.

Nor did she say, "*Wolf* is a dumb name for a dog." Or: "*Dunk* is a dumb name for a boy."

She just looked through Dunk as if he weren't even there.

Dunk flushed a dull red.

"Well, here's a cupcake for *that* dumb cat," he said.

He thrust his cupcake toward Emma's cat sweater. Emma shrieked, not a happy shriek but the same terrified shriek she had given at the sight of Nora's ant farm.

Startled, Dunk dropped the cupcake. It landed, frosting side down, on Emma's favorite flouncy skirt.

"I hate you, Dunk!" Emma burst into tears just as Coach Joe came over to their pod, saying, "Team, team. What's going on?"

At least the cupcake hadn't gotten on Emma's sweater cat, the cat that nobody was allowed to touch without proof of clean hands.

But that was little consolation as Emma sat crying and Dunk looked as if he was about to cry, too.

Male ants live a much shorter time than females—only a few weeks or months. Most of them do no work at all! I'm not saying this to be critical of boy ants. This is just a fact.

Nora wore a dress to Emma's high tea for Precious Cupcake, but she drew the line at a hat. The only hats she owned were warm stocking caps for the winter and canvas hats with sun visors for the summer, plus one old-fashioned sunbonnet her parents had bought her at a crafts fair. She tried the sunbonnet on just to see how it looked with her dress, but then she took it off again. It made her look like a pioneer girl from *Little House on the Prairie*, not a typical guest at an elegant tea party. Of course, Precious Cupcake wasn't going to look like a typical guest at an elegant tea party, either.

"My, don't you look pretty," her mother commented as Nora came downstairs right before the party.

Nora made a face. Whenever she wore a dress, people always made a point of telling her that she looked pretty.

Had people ever told Marie Curie, discoverer of radium, that she looked pretty?

Did they tell Jane Goodall, the world's foremost expert on chimpanzees, that she looked pretty?

Nora greatly doubted it.

Her mother drove her to Emma's house.

"How long do you think it would take a piece of mail to get from Colorado to New York?" Nora asked her mother. She had mailed her ant article to *Nature* on Thursday, and now it was Sunday.

"Two days?" her mother guessed. "Why?"

"I was just wondering," Nora said.

"That's one of the things I love most about you," her mother told her. "You're always wondering about something."

If Nora's mother was right, her ant article would have arrived yesterday, Saturday. The editors at

Nature probably didn't work on the weekend. Or maybe they did? Her scientist parents worked as hard on weekends as they did during the week. Say they got it Saturday and sent it off right away to the big ant expert. The ant expert would get it on—Tuesday? And read it on Wednesday. And send the review off on Thursday. The editors would get the review back on Saturday.

There was no way she was going to hear anything in less than a week. More likely two or even three, in case the ant expert was busy with other things, like grading exams for his ant students or writing ant papers of his own.

His or *her* own.

"How are you supposed to act at a fancy tea party?" Nora asked her mother as they pulled into Emma's long, curved driveway.

"Actually," her mother said, "I don't believe I've ever been to a fancy tea party. You'll have to tell *me* when you get home. Just follow Emma's lead."

Well, if Nora followed Emma's lead, she'd be spending most of the tea party fussing over Precious Cupcake.

"Have fun!" her mother told her.

"I'll try," Nora replied.

The first thing Nora noticed, when she caught a glimpse of the other guests through the double doors leading into Emma's dining room, was that they were all wearing hats. The hats looked like Easter bonnets, not that Nora had ever seen an Easter bonnet in real life. Their dresses were covered with lace, ruffles, and bows.

Nora's own dress was plain and simple. It looked sporty, not poofy, more like a dress you could play basketball in, if anybody ever played basketball wearing a dress. More like a dress an ant scientist would wear.

Emma looked worried as she took Nora's coat.

"Would you like to borrow a hat?" she asked in a low voice, so the girls in the other room wouldn't hear. "I have a hat that would look great with your dress. Kind of, you know, dress it up a bit?"

Nora hesitated. She'd feel strange, un-Nora-like, if she borrowed Emma's hat. But she already felt un-Nora-like being at Emma's tea party in the first place. And her mother *had* told her to follow Emma's lead.

"Sure," Nora said.

Emma darted upstairs and returned a moment later with a hat for Nora. The hat was made of lavender straw, with a huge, floppy yellow flower on one side, as big as a sunflower, but definitely not a sunflower. Nora was pretty sure it was a flower unknown to botanists, a flower found nowhere in the natural world.

Ridiculous hat perched bravely on her head, Nora caught a glimpse of herself in the small, round mirror on the wall leading to the dining room.

Oh well.

Emma's mother appeared, as dressed up as her daughter, also wearing a hat.

"Why, Nora," she said. "Don't you look pretty!"

Nora forced herself to smile.

"I love your hat! I believe Emma has one almost exactly like it. That yellow flower is just darling!"

Nora made her smile even wider.

Emma's dining room table was covered with a long white tablecloth. Seven places were set with strawberry-patterned plates and matching teacups and saucers. Nora saw that each place was marked with a flowered name card written in a graceful cursive that had to have been done by Emma's mother.

Nora found hers: Miss Nora Alpers.

As the six girls took their seats, Nora saw that one seat was still empty—the seat at her left—where the chair was piled high with cushions.

Its name card read: Miss Precious Cupcake.

"Where *is* Precious Cupcake?" Bethy asked. "Doesn't she know the whole party is for *her*?"

"The guest of honor always arrives *last*," Emma informed Bethy.

"Oh," Bethy said. "I didn't know."

As if on cue, Emma's older sister, wearing a black dress with a frilly white apron and matching frilly white cap, entered, cradling Precious Cupcake in her arms. Nora had thought Precious Cupcake might be wearing the same pink cape and silver tiara she had displayed in the "Princess Precious" cat video, but the cat had a new outfit Nora had never seen before. This time, it was an actual dress, just like a girl's dress, pink with embroidered strawberries all over it and a pink satiny ribbon tied around it. The outfit was topped off by a hat with a large yellow flower that looked to be the same genus and species as the flower on Nora's hat.

A hush fell over the guests at the table.

Then:

"Ooh!"

"Aww!"

"She's sooooo cute!"

"She's the cutest ever!"

Nora widened her already wide smile.

"Nora," Elise said, "her flower looks just like yours!"

"It does!" Tamara agreed.

"You're the Precious Cupcake twins!" Bethy said.

Nora's face was starting to ache from smiling.

Emma's sister set Precious Cupcake on the chair of honor. Nora expected the cat to leap away and scurry for shelter. But Precious Cupcake stayed at her royal post as if she attended fancy tea parties all the time and knew exactly how to behave.

Maybe Nora could just follow the cat's lead now.

"May I pour you some tea?" Emma asked, gesturing toward the silver teapot her mother had just placed on the table.

"Yes, please!" came a chorus of replies.

"Let me help with the pouring," Emma's mother offered. "The tea is very hot. Girls, I hope you all like strawberry herbal tea."

"Strawberry, to match the strawberries on the plates," Emma explained. "And the strawberries on Precious Cupcake's dress."

Emma's sister was serving as party waitress. Her little frilly apron and cap must be her waitress costume. She now appeared carrying two silver trays, one balanced on each hand.

"Cucumber sandwiches and scones," Emma announced. "There's clotted cream—that's the white stuff in the little bowl—and lemon curd—that's the yellow stuff—and raspberry preserves—that's a fancy word for jam. Oh, that reminds me. We all need to start talking in a fancy way."

"Like people in the olden days?" Elise asked. "Like, instead of saying, *I would like some more tea,* say, *I would liketh some more tea.*"

For the first time since her guests had arrived, Emma looked unsure. "Well, maybe."

"And say *thee* and *thou,*" Elise added. She was the biggest reader of any of the girls at the table, except for Nora. But Nora didn't tend to read books about people who said *thee* and *thou.* "Would thou pourest me some tea?" Elise said, as an example to show the other girls.

Emma plainly didn't like having anything at her

tea party dictated by someone else. "Well, I don't think we need to go *that* far," she said.

"How about, thou *can* talketh that way, but thou doesn't *have* to," Tamara suggested.

"Okay then," Emma agreed grudgingly. "That sounds—I mean, that soundeth—good."

Emma's sister arrived with yet another silver tray, this one filled with tiny pink-frosted cupcakes, each one topped with a sliver of real strawberry.

"Emma, I loveth this tea party!" Elise said.

"I'm glad you love it," Emma said. "I mean, that thou loveth it."

Nora helped herself to a cucumber sandwich, scone, and cupcake. She tried a bite of scone with clotted cream and raspberry preserves. It was delicious. She was relieved to see that Precious Cupcake was served different, species-appropriate treats: a dollop of wet cat food on a strawberry-patterned saucer, and part of what smelled like an anchovy.

"So, Emma," Bethy said. "Tell us. Does thou hatest Dunk now?"

Emma's face darkened. "I do! I do hateth him. Because he hateth Precious Cupcake, and he almost ruineth my favorite sweater."

"I hate *all* boys," Elise declared. "What about the rest of you? Do you hateth all boys, too?"

Nora was glad to see that *thou* had apparently been dropped from the conversation. She couldn't imagine how Elise could have asked that same question with *thou* in it. *What about the rest of thous? Do thous hateth all boys, too?* Even though she hadn't read any books with *thee* and *thou* in them, she knew that couldn't possibly be right.

"Yes!" the other girls all answered.

"What about you, Nora?" Bethy asked. "Do you hate all boys, too?"

Even to follow Emma's lead, Nora couldn't lie. "No. I like Mason. I like Brody. It doesn't make sense to hate *all* boys or *all* dogs or *all* cats or *all* of anything."

"So do you *like* like Mason? Or *like* like Brody?" Elise persisted. "If I didn't hate all boys, I might not hate Brody."

Nora didn't feel like talking anymore about hating or *like* liking boys. But Emma wasn't going to let Elise's question drop.

"So do you, Nora? *Like* like Mason or Brody?"

"No."

Desperately, Nora looked around for something else to talk about besides boys or Precious Cupcake, who, she saw, was still sitting nicely in her place, the perfect guest in every respect.

Except for one.

Precious Cupcake was just now swallowing the pink ribbon from her pink cat dress.

"Emma!" Nora cried. "Precious Cupcake!"

All eyes turned to the cat as the last tip of pink ribbon disappeared down her throat.

Some ants can snap their jaws shut so fast that it's one of the fastest body-part movements ever recorded in the animal kingdom. Precious Cupcake didn't swallow her ribbon that fast. But she definitely swallowed it faster than I could think to stop her.

That was the end of high tea.

Emma sat sobbing, hugging Precious Cupcake even as she kept crying, "Bad cat! Bad cat!" Emma's mother called the vet, and they said to take Precious Cupcake to urgent veterinary care because a long swallowed ribbon could cause a blockage in a cat's intestines. The vet said that Precious Cupcake might need surgery. Emma sobbed even harder.

"Oh, Precious Cupcake, how could you?" she moaned.

All the girls, including Nora, crowded around

Emma to try to comfort her, but Emma couldn't be comforted.

Emma's mother loaded a loudly meowing Precious Cupcake into the cat carrier. Nora could see that it had what looked like a velvet cushion inside. Then Emma and her mother left for the vet. Emma's sister, still in her lacy waitress apron and cap, stayed while the guests called their parents for rides home. It was only at the last minute that Nora remembered that she was still wearing Emma's flowered hat. She set it on the front hall table, her head free at last.

"So how was it?" her mother asked in the car on the way home. "Except for poor Precious Cupcake, of course."

"It was okay." The scone had been tasty, even though Nora hadn't been able to finish it with all the commotion over Cupcake's catastrophe. "I didn't really liketh it, but I didn't hateth it, either."

"Liketh? Hateth?"

"*That's* what people do at fancy tea parties," Nora told her. "They talk in a fancy way."

"Oh," her mother said. "Well, now we know."

Emma's vet decided that Precious Cupcake should be observed for twenty-four hours to see if the ribbon "emerges from the other end." That was what Emma told the girls at lunch on Monday.

"Emerges from the other end?" Elise asked.

"You know," Amy said, with veterinary authority. "The *other* end."

"Ewww!" said Tamara.

"Gross!" said Bethy.

"Is someone going to have to *check*?" Elise wanted to know. "Ick!"

125

Emma plainly didn't like having the words *ewww, gross,* and *ick* applied in any way to Precious Cupcake. She drew herself up erect and glared at her friends.

Nora didn't understand how the other girls could be so grossed out by an ordinary bodily function they themselves performed every day. Mason and Brody cleaned up after Dog. Emma probably scooped out the litter box, or someone in her family did. Nora's own ants carefully dealt with their waste, keeping it separate in a special area of the ant farm. What was *ewww, gross,* or *ick* about it?

"It's better than making her have surgery," Nora pointed out, trying to turn the conversation in a sensible direction. Amy nodded in agreement.

But the cries of *ewww, gross,* and *ick* had already drawn Dunk to their table, an eager glint in his eye. If there was anyone who was an expert in things that could be described in that way, it was Dunk.

"What happened?" he asked, hopeful. "What's gross?"

"Don't tell him," Emma commanded.

But Bethy couldn't resist. "Precious Cupcake swallowed a ribbon, and now Emma has to wait and see if it—well—if it—you know—comes out the other end."

"If she *poops* it out?" Dunk practically shouted. He burst into the loudest guffaws Nora had heard from him yet.

Emma turned on him with a look of the fiercest rage Nora had seen from her yet.

"My cat might have to have an operation!" she spat out. "My cat might die!"

Nora thought Emma was exaggerating just a bit, for effect.

"Swallowing a ribbon can be fatal to cats! You think that's *funny*? If my cat dies, you're going to *laugh*?"

Poor Dunk, Nora thought. This was even worse than trying to smush his frosted cupcake onto Emma's cat sweater.

For the first time, Dunk seemed to get it.

"I don't want—" he stammered. "I just—I mean—poop is funny. Isn't it?"

All of the girls now stared at him with utter disdain.

Dunk's lower lip quivered. "I don't want your cat to die!" he blubbered.

Emma continued to freeze him with her stare, until finally Dunk slunk away back to his own table. Bethy put her arm around Emma's shaking shoulders.

"What if Precious Cupcake does die?" Emma whispered.

Elise's eyes glistened.

Tamara wiped away a tear.

Nora had had all she could take. "She's not going to die." She looked over at Amy, who nodded.

"How do you know?" Bethy shot back.

"I don't *know*," Nora said. "But it's very unlikely. Pets swallow things they shouldn't all the time. Usually those things pass right through them."

"That's right," Amy agreed. "And pets have operations all the time and come through them just fine."

But the other girls were obviously in the mood to be sad. Nora couldn't help but think it was all partly a show to make Dunk feel even worse than he did already.

She sighed and finished eating her ham and cheese sandwich. Someone had to stay calm, cool, and collected. And, as often as not, she was that someone.

At home that evening, Nora was curled up on the family room couch, busy at work on her persuasive speech, her ants beside her, busy with another ant funeral. A lot of them had been dying lately. Nora knew as well as anyone that a colony without a queen couldn't survive forever.

But she didn't let herself dwell on that unpleasant thought. She had to focus on her speech, which was due on Friday, just four days away.

She had decided to pull all of her ideas together and write about how more people should study science, especially girls. She had looked up statistics on what percentage of PhD degrees in science was awarded to women: not a very big one. If only more people studied science, more people would care about all the amazing creatures of the world, many of them endangered now by loss of habitat and climate change. If only more people, especially girls like Emma, studied science, they might even appreciate ants.

At seven-thirty, the phone rang. Nora picked it up.

The caller didn't identify herself, but Nora knew right away who it was and what the call was about.

It was a girl.

And the girl said, "It came out!"

So Nora had been correct, after all.

Precious Cupcake was going to be just fine.

One of the greatest perils ants face in nature is drought. I make sure to give my ants enough water so they are never thirsty. An experiment I'm not going to try: if I gave them part of a ribbon to eat, would they eat it?

13

Nora had already calculated that the soonest she could possibly hear from *Nature* about her ant article would be next week. And she could hear by next week only if the big ant expert dropped everything else, pounced upon her article, and read it right away.

But as soon as she got home from school on Wednesday, her father, who was working at home, handed her a letter.

"You got something from *Nature*," he said, looking puzzled. "How on earth would they have gotten your name and address? It doesn't look like a mass mailing, either. It looks like a letter sent just to you."

Stalling for time, Nora studied the envelope, addressed to Miss Nora Alpers.

Her father stood waiting for her to open it. Her parents would never open a piece of mail addressed to somebody else. They believed in privacy. But her father might as well have opened her letter, as he plainly planned on standing there until he found out what it said.

Well, she had been planning to tell him sooner or later. It might as well be sooner.

But today was too soon. Even the speediest ant expert couldn't possibly have had time to review her article yet.

"Aren't you going to open it?" her father said.

Nora picked up the fancy silver letter opener her parents kept on the front hall table and slid it under the flap of the envelope. She drew out the one sheet of paper inside. The paper was thick and fancy, with *Nature* printed at the top.

She started reading.

Dear Miss Alpers:

Thank you for sending us your article, "The Ants Go Marching—Until They Reach the Chalk Line!" We are impressed that you have such a serious scientific interest in ants at your age.

We are unable to publish this in <u>Nature</u>, but we hope you will send us other articles when you are older. We wish you all the best with your future career in science.

The letter was signed at the bottom with an illegible scrawl from the editor.

"So?" her father asked.

"They rejected it," Nora said in a small voice. "I wrote an article about my ants, and I sent it to them, and they said to try again when I'm *older.*"

Nora didn't tell him that she had been trying to break the Guinness World Record for youngest person to publish an article in a grown-up science journal. That goal now seemed as ridiculous as Brody's thinking he could get Dog to hold the most tennis balls in his mouth or walk the longest distance with a glass of water on his head.

Who was she to think she could break a world record for anything?

"You sent an article to *Nature*?" her father asked, even though that was what she had already told him.

She handed him the letter so he could read it himself.

"I don't think they even showed it to the big ant expert," she whispered.

"What big ant expert?"

"*You* know. You said they send the articles off to big experts. But I think they just wrote me back right away. Because I'm a kid. And I didn't even tell them I was ten. They just guessed. Even though I typed it up and everything. And made graphs! In color!"

Nora wasn't going to cry in front of her father. She wasn't. If she had to cry, she was going to do it later, alone with her ants.

"Honey," her father said, "I think it's wonderful that you tried to publish your article. How many ten-year-olds would even try?"

"An eleven-year-old girl tried and succeeded," Nora shot back. "Her name was Emily Rosa. She's in the *Guinness World Records* book."

"An eleven-year-old published an article in *Nature*?" her father asked, sounding incredulous.

"No, not in *Nature*, but it was in some grown-up science journal."

"Well, sweetie, some journals are easier to publish in than others. *Nature* is one of the very hardest. It might be too much to expect to publish in the *very* top journals right away. And even though you've been learning so much about ants, you only spent a few days on your experiment, right? Some scientists work on their experiments for years. For decades, even."

"So I was silly to try. Is that what you're saying?"

"No. It's never silly to try. Everything that has ever happened in the history of science happened because of someone who tried to learn something new about this amazing, fascinating, incredibly complex world of ours."

Nora knew her father wanted to make her feel better.

But she didn't feel better. She didn't feel better at all.

Upstairs in her room, she didn't want to look at her ants. Even the sight of their busy scurrying and tunneling wasn't going to cheer up a ten-year-old who was too young to be taken seriously by her fellow ant scientists.

How could they not think it was interesting and important that ants wouldn't cross a chalk line unless they had an important reason to cross it? She had probably proven single-handedly that ants could not only react to the world around them by instinct but also actually *think*.

Maybe it was her handwriting on the envelope that had given her away. Her cursive didn't look like her parents' cursive. It looked like the handwriting of someone who had spent two weeks in third grade in a unit on how to write in cursive. Or maybe the title of her article wasn't catchy, but dumb. After all, she had thought it was dumb when Coach Joe had sung "The Ants Go Marching" the day she had brought her ant farm to school, the day the other girls had screamed and run away.

She blinked back the tears she hadn't let herself cry in front of her father.

Maybe her ants *would* make her feel better. Her

ants didn't know or care that she was only ten. They didn't care that her cursive looked like writing by some kid. They didn't care that she—that *they*—had just been ignored by the editor of a famous science journal.

She walked over to her ant farm to see what they were up to. But then her heart sank. Right now, actually, her ants didn't look as if they knew or cared about much of anything.

The ant farm was strangely still.

Two ants were busy in one of the tunnels, but their activity looked aimless, as if they had lost their way, as if they weren't sure what they were supposed to be doing anymore or why they were supposed to be doing it.

She looked more closely.

The rest of the ants were completely motionless.

Sleeping? All of them?

Or dead?

Some ant queens produce as many daughters as there are people in the whole United States. But only a few million are alive at any time. Ants die a LOT.

Nora had had ants die before.

Dying was one of the things ants did.

This time felt different, though.

These were the ants she had tried to show to her unappreciative classmates. These were the ants that had led to an important scientific discovery that might have even proved that ants could think.

Nora didn't just love ants in general.

She loved these ants in particular.

But they were definitely dead, all but two of them.

Nora hadn't known that the deaths of creatures so small could leave so big a hole in her heart.

During the morning huddle on Friday, Coach Joe asked who wanted to share their persuasive speeches. Brody's hand was first to shoot in the air, as usual. But this time, to Nora's great surprise, Mason raised his hand, too. Nora decided to volunteer as well. After all, what was the point of a persuasive speech if you didn't use it to try to persuade somebody?

"Great!" Coach Joe said. "Brody, you're up at bat first."

"I changed mine," Brody explained before he started reading. "I was going to write about the colonists and how they shouldn't have a war, but just try to work things out instead. And I did write about that. But then I added something else. About a different war. A war right here in our own class."

Brody's eyes swept the huddle, as if to make sure that everyone was ready to be persuaded of something very important.

"Okay, Brody," Coach Joe said. "Let's hear it."

Don't Have Any Wars
By Brody Baxter

War is a very bad idea. It is always better not to have a war if possible. Whenever there is a war, one side wins and one side loses. But really both sides lose.

The American colonists were mad at the British because their taxes were too high. They were mad because they had to pay taxes on stamps. Then they got even madder because they had to pay taxes on tea. If there was one thing people loved long ago, it was drinking tea. Plus, they were mad because they didn't get to vote on any of these taxes. They thought it wasn't fair to have taxation without representation.

So they started a war. The war did make America free from the British. But thousands of people died on both sides. The soldiers were miserable during the cold winters. They had to walk in the snow with no shoes. The war cost a lot of money, too.

If King George the Third had just let the colonies be their own country, it would have saved lots of lives and lots of money, and the ending would have been just the same. If the colonists had tried to get along better with the British, sooner or later the British would have gotten tired of having colonies anyway. Nobody has colonies anymore today.

So they shouldn't have had a war.

In our own class, we've been having a war of cat people against dog people. The war is hurting a lot of people's feelings. There is no need to have a war in our class. Dog people can love dogs best, but they can still like cats, too. Cat people can love cats best, but they can still like dogs, too. And if they don't, they can just keep quiet and not say mean things about other people's pets.

If the British and Americans hadn't had a war, they could have all been happy.

If cat lovers and dog lovers in our class stop their war, we can all be happy, too.

Brody looked up from his paper with a huge grin.

"Thanks, Brody," Coach Joe said. "I think a lot of us needed to hear that. So, team, is anybody persuaded?"

The huddle burst into applause.

Nora saw Dunk, blushing brick red, whisper something to Emma.

Emma giggled and whispered something back.

Dunk whispered something else.

Emma giggled again.

"Oh, Dunk!" Nora heard her say.

Apparently, Brody's speech had brought about at least one truce in the dog-cat war.

"Mason," Coach Joe said then. "What do you have for us? What do you want to persuade us of?"

Mason began reading:

A Persuasive Speech Against Persuasive Speeches
By Mason Dixon

In our class at school, we are learning how to write persuasive speeches. We are learning how to persuade other people to think and act the way we want them to. I think that before we learn how to persuade people, we should ask ourselves if that is a good thing to do. I say no.

The first reason we shouldn't try to persuade people is that people have a right to think the way they want to think and to do the things they want to do. As long as it doesn't hurt anybody else. Why should everybody think the same way? It's good that people think lots of different things.

The second reason we shouldn't try to persuade people is that it doesn't work. People just decide to keep believing the first thing they believed, only harder. When someone tries too hard to sell something to you, you get suspicious. It makes you want not to buy that thing even more.

The third reason we shouldn't try to persuade people is that it is irritating. In fact, it is very irritating. If someone doesn't like to do new things, and other people, like that person's parents, keep telling him to try new things, that person is going to get irritated and want the other people to stop. If that person only likes brown socks, and macaroni and cheese, and Fig Newtons, that person isn't going to like being told over and over again to wear other-color socks and eat other foods.

So, in conclusion, people shouldn't try to persuade other people. The end.

"Good one!" Coach Joe said once Mason stopped reading. "I never thought of things that way. Team, what do you think?"

Lots of kids clapped this time, too.

"Yup," Coach Joe said. "I think Mason hit that one right out of the ballpark."

A boy named James read an anti-homework persuasive speech. Nora liked that it quoted statistics, which claimed that there was no relationship between how much homework students did at night and how well they scored on standardized tests. She adored statistics. Then a girl named Hazel read a persuasive speech about some celebrity who wore too much makeup and how she would look better with less makeup. That one was dopey, in Nora's opinion. People either liked makeup or didn't, the same way some people liked dogs and some people liked cats. Amy read her speech, which turned out to be about how people in the U.S. should keep pet cats indoors so that they wouldn't keep killing over 2 billion songbirds each year. Nora remembered that, fortunately, Precious Cupcake was already an indoor cat.

"Nora?" Coach Joe called on her.

She picked up her paper and started to read.

The Importance of Studying Science
By Nora Alpers

Many people I know think science is a boring subject. In fact, some of these people are girls in my class at school. Even when girls think science is interesting, they can feel like they're not supposed to, because the other girls they know talk more about boys, clothes, or cats, instead of about batteries, planets, and ants.

This pattern continues when girls grow up. More than half the people in America are female, but less than a quarter of scientists, engineers, mathematicians, and tech workers are women. Only one-fifth of physics PhDs are given to women. Only fourteen percent of physics professors are women. In a whole century, only fifteen women got a Nobel Prize in science.

These are very sad facts, because it is so important that everybody, including girls, knows about science. We need to know about science so that we can protect our planet. Species are going extinct at a faster rate than any other time in human history, because of things that humans do. People do things that cause climate change and loss of habitat. If people knew more about science, they would know not to do these things. More important, if people knew more about science, they wouldn't *want* to do these things. The more you learn about science, the more interesting and important you think everything in the world is. Even little tiny things that most people don't care about, like ants.

So it is important for everybody to learn about science, but especially for girls, because they are getting left out right now. My family is full of women scientists. My mother is a scientist who is an expert on the rings of Saturn. My sister is a scientist who studies rock formations. I want to be a scientist, too, and learn as much as I can about ants.

Even if you don't want to be a scientist, I hope you learn as much as you can about science. Science may not be "cute," but it is interesting, beautiful, and important for our world. The more we all learn about science, the more we can save our world.

Nora took a deep breath when she was done. What would her classmates think? She knew Amy would like it. But would the rest of them be persuaded?

They were all clapping loudly. But they had applauded every speech so far, even the dumb one about celebrity makeup. She doubted that she had actually persuaded anybody, not the way that Brody had. But then, as Coach Joe was closing the huddle by saying something about seeing if the local newspaper might want to publish any of their speeches, Emma leaned over to her.

"I'm sorry, Nora," Emma said. "I shouldn't have screamed that day when your ants came to school. I was definitely being unscientific. I hope you bring your ants to school again sometime soon. I really do."

Even though Nora knew Emma meant well, this

request, following upon the rejection of her ant article *and* the collapse of her entire ant colony, was too much for her to bear.

"I can't," Nora snapped. "They're dead."

"Dead?" Emma asked, as if she couldn't have heard correctly.

"Yes," Nora said brightly. "All of them." The last two had died yesterday. "But thanks for asking."

Before Emma could make any reply, Nora marched off to her desk, took out her math book, and made herself very busy converting fractions to decimals.

In almost every ant colony, once the queen dies, the whole colony dies, ant by ant by ant. Ant colonies die just as individual ants do. But when they die, it's a lot sadder.

15

At lunch, Nora was surprised to see Dunk approach the table with his tray, a sheepish grin on his face.

"I'm here," he said to Emma.

Tamara was absent that day. Emma motioned to Dunk to take Tamara's empty seat.

Nora took notice. A fourth-grade boy was sitting at a fourth-grade girls' cafeteria table. To her knowledge, that had never happened before at Plainfield Elementary School.

"Dunk," Emma announced to the other girls,

"told me that he's interested in seeing some of Precious Cupcake's cat videos."

Dunk made a strangled sound. Nora could tell that he wanted to say that he wasn't *interested* in watching cat videos, but that he had reluctantly agreed to watch them as part of the truce between cat people and dog people. Nora could also tell that he knew better than to point that out.

"Are you ready?" Emma asked him sweetly.

Dunk grunted.

"Girls, which one should I show him first?"

"'Princess Precious,'" Bethy said.

"'Cupcake Capers'!" Elise answered.

"They're all adorable," Amy said, in case there had been any hard feelings over her anti-bird-eating speech.

"Nora?" Emma asked.

Nora knew Emma was trying to be extra-friendly to make up for the deaths of her ants.

"Do you have any videos from the high tea?" Nora asked, because she couldn't think of anything else. "I mean, from the high tea before she swallowed the ribbon?"

As soon as she said it, she realized it was the wrong thing to have said.

"I'll start with 'Princess Precious,'" Emma declared.

She fiddled with her phone for a minute as Dunk shoveled in some hasty mouthfuls of hamburger casserole.

"All right!" Emma chirped. "Here's the first one!"

Dunk put down his fork. Nobody was supposed to watch videos of Precious Cupcake with divided attention.

Emma and Dunk leaned their heads together so they could look at the cat videos at the same time. The other girls got up from their seats and crowded behind them, even though Nora couldn't begin to count how many times they had seen them all before.

"Ohh!"

"So cute!"

"The cutest!"

That, from the girls.

Dunk hadn't yet said anything.

"Dunk, you're supposed to say *ooh* and *aah*," Emma instructed.

Already red, Dunk grew even redder. But there was no halfway point for admiration of Emma's cat videos.

"Ooh," he muttered sullenly. "Aah."

"Say how cute she is," Emma commanded.

Nora wondered if Dunk would bolt back to his own table, where two boys were having a lively duel with their bread sticks.

He didn't.

"She *is* cute," he said, sounding surprised, and surprisingly sincere.

Emma giggled.

"Now let me find the one where she's licking the cupcake frosting. Oh, here it is!"

Dunk gave another grunt of appreciation.

Emma giggled again.

The weekend was a long, empty one, without any ants in it.

Saturday morning, Nora emptied the contents of the ant farm into the backyard, all the sad remains of the formerly bustling ant colony. She set her ant farm on a dusty shelf in the back of the garage.

"You aren't getting any more ants?" her mother asked as they were getting ready to head over to the last Fighting Bulldogs game of the season.

"No," Nora told her. "I'm through with ants."

"You're through with *ants*?"

Why did Nora always have to repeat everything? Didn't people listen the first time? But she knew her mother had heard her; her mother just didn't believe her.

"You never liked my ants anyway," Nora said. It came out sounding like an accusation.

"That's not true."

"It is true. Admit it."

"Okay, I never liked having *stinging* ants *loose* in my kitchen. That much is true. But I definitely liked your ants when they were safe in their farm."

Nora must have looked skeptical, because her mother went on, "Well, I always liked that *you* liked your ants. Your father and I are both so proud of you for being such a serious scientist, studying your ants, doing experiments with them. How many girls your age are already budding myrmecologists? In fact, your father told me that you—"

Nora cut her off with a glare that said, *Don't even go there*. She couldn't stand to hear her mother trying to be like her father and make it sound wonderful that she had even tried to publish her ant article. She didn't want credit for *trying*. She wanted credit for *succeeding*.

"Anyway, we're proud of you," her mother finished.

The Bulldogs won their game. Nora scored the winning basket.

Mason, Brody, and the rest of their teammates were all screaming with excitement when the buzzer sounded.

"Nora! Nora! Nora!" they cheered.

It was amazing how worked up people could get about things that didn't really matter.

After the game, Nora went home to a house with no ants for her to check on. She didn't have any homework to do. Coach Joe had said that in honor of the anti-homework persuasive speech, he'd give them one weekend with no homework at all.

Nora didn't feel like calling Mason and Brody. They were probably busy teaching Dog new tricks or giving him another bath to try to get rid of the last, lingering skunk odor.

She didn't feel like calling any of the girls, even

Amy. They were probably busy talking about how funny Dunk had looked watching Emma's cat videos and how the cat videos really were the cutest videos in the history of the world. Amy would be busy with her whole household full of still-living pets.

She didn't feel like disturbing her parents. They were both hunched over the computers in their home offices, probably busy writing articles to be published in prestigious grown-up science journals.

She didn't feel like doing anything.

Monday morning, Nora found a pale blue envelope on her desk. Her name was written on it in round printing that could only have been done by a girl. The *o* in *Nora* had petals around it to form a flower.

The envelope contained a card with a picture of a rainbow on the front of it, with fancy script that read:

With Deepest Sympathy on the Loss of Your Pets

Someone had added an *s* to *Pet* to make it read *Pets*.

Inside the card was a printed poem:

> *Pets are angels in disguise.*
> *They give us joy and love.*
> *When they finally pass away,*
> *They watch us from above.*
>
> *From Heaven your pets are looking down*
> *And sent me here to say*
> *The love they give is never lost*
> *But still with you today.*

The card was signed: Emma.

Nora didn't know whether to cry or laugh.

As much as she missed her ants, she couldn't think of them as angels, even as *very* well-disguised angels.

She didn't think they were in heaven watching her and hoping Emma would give her a card about them.

She had loved her ants. But she couldn't honestly say that they had loved her back.

That wasn't what ants *did*.

"Huddle time!" Coach Joe called out. "Hurry on over, team. I have some good news to share."

Nora found a place next to Mason and Brody.

"My parents read my anti-persuasive persuasive speech," Mason told her.

"And?"

"They weren't persuaded."

Nora laughed.

"Actually, they were sort of persuaded. My mom said I still have to try new foods sometimes. And go new places. But I don't have to do figure skating! And I don't have to take voice lessons. My dad looked pretty thrilled about it. I don't think he wanted to have to listen to me practice."

Nora laughed again.

"All right, team," Coach Joe said. "Here's today's paper, hot off the press: the *Plainfield Daily Record*."

Nora's parents got the *Plainfield Daily Record*, but they hadn't had time to read it this morning.

"Well, on the op-ed page today—that's the page *opposite* the *editorial* page—there is a piece by one of our classmates. A persuasive speech about the importance of getting more kids, especially girls, to study science. Congratulations, Nora!"

Nora was bewildered. But then she remembered that Coach Joe had said something about seeing if the newspaper might want to publish their speeches. Apparently, they had. And the one they wanted to publish was hers.

This time, the applause from her classmates was more than polite. It sounded more like the cheers of the Fighting Bulldogs after she had scored the winning basket.

Her persuasive speech wasn't published in *Nature*. It wasn't going to set any Guinness World Record for youngest article by anyone ever. But right now it felt pretty sweet to have Coach Joe hold up the newspaper, folded open to the page where her article appeared, framed in a little box:

THE IMPORTANCE OF STUDYING SCIENCE
By Nora Alpers

Nora is a fourth-grade student
at Plainfield Elementary School.

Part of her wished they hadn't printed her grade. Maybe they had published her article because it was good for a fourth grader, not because it was good, period.

Then again, she *was* a fourth grader. And the newspaper editors obviously thought it was impressive that a fourth grader had written an article good enough to be published.

When the applause had died down, Coach Joe said, "So, Nora, speaking of getting kids more interested in science, what do you think? Will you give us another chance with your ant farm?"

Nora heard Emma's gasp.

"Coach Joe," Emma blurted out, "Nora can't bring her ant farm in again. Because, you see, her ants are—well, they're . . ." She lowered her voice to avoid saying the final word too loudly. "They're *deceased.*"

Coach Joe turned to Nora, as if to confirm the truth of this terrible statement.

Nora thought for a moment before speaking.

"My ants did die. My colony didn't have a queen, and without a queen, a colony dies out in a few weeks or months. That's the life span of the worker ants. But it's okay when ants die. It's part of the life cycle. Ants go through four different stages in their lives: egg, larva, pupa, adult. Once they're adults, they do their work to help the colony survive. Then they die. It's what ants *do*."

She looked around at her classmates, all of them seeming to be listening hard to every word she spoke, even Dunk. Maybe next, Dunk would be agreeing to watch ant videos.

"I'm going to get more ants soon," Nora told the class.

Had she really just said that? Apparently, she had.

"It's winter now, so I don't think I can find any outside in nature. Maybe next summer, I can find more ants in my backyard and even find a queen to go with them. But for now, I can send away on-line to get more ants shipped to me in the mail. I'll bring them in once I get them."

She hadn't spoken the truth to her mother, even though she had thought what she said was true at the time.

She wasn't through with ants.

She was never going to be through with ants.

She'd always want to study ants and learn about them. Maybe she *would* publish an article in

Nature someday, when she had studied ants for years and years.

She was going to study ants forever.

After all, studying ants was what Nora *did*.

Fascinating ant fact:

There are only 500 myrmecologists in the world.

Counting me, 501!

ACKNOWLEDGMENTS

It is a joy to be able to thank some of the wonderful people who helped bring this book into being. It was during breakfast with my brilliant editor, Nancy Hinkel, that I paid attention when she said, "I could use a book about a girl with an ant farm!" Her encouragement and enthusiasm fueled Nora's love of ants on every page. I received careful critique on early drafts from my longtime Boulder writing group (Marie DesJardin, Mary Peace Finley, Ann Whitehead Nagda, Leslie O'Kane, Phyllis Perry, and Elizabeth Wrenn). Professor Whitney Cranshaw of Colorado State University gave generously of his time and expertise to talk with me about ants (any ant-related errors in the book are, of course, my own). I looked at Katie Kath's adorable first sketches for the book and said, "There she is! There's Nora!"

Thanks also to my wise and caring agent, Stephen Fraser; consistently helpful Stephen Brown; magnificently sharp-eyed copy editors Esther Lin, Steph Engel, and Artie Bennett; and Isabel Warren-Lynch and Trish Parcell for their appealing book design.

Most of Nora's fascinating ant facts are drawn from *Journey to the Ants: A Story of Scientific Exploration* by Bert Hölldobler and Edward O. Wilson, Cambridge, Mass.: Belknap Press, 1994. On behalf of Nora and all budding myrmecologists everywhere, I am grateful to them for this amazing book.

Claudia Mills is the author of over fifty books for young readers, including the Mason Dixon series. She does not personally keep an ant farm, but she does have a cat, Snickers, with whom she curls up on her couch at home in Boulder, Colorado, drinking hot chocolate and writing. Visit her at claudiamillsauthor.com.